The Indigenous Compositions

Edited by: Kuntala Bhattacharya

Ukiyoto Publishing

All global publishing rights are held by

Ukiyoto Publishing

Published in 2021

Content Copyright © **Kuntala Bhattacharya**

ISBN9789364946308

All rights reserved.
No part of this publication may be reproduced, transmitted, or stored in a retrieval system, in any form by any means, electronic, mechanical, photocopying, recording or otherwise, without the prior permission of the publisher.

The moral rights of the author have been asserted.

This is a work of fiction. Names, characters, businesses, places, events, locales, and incidents are either the products of the author's imagination or used in a fictitious manner. Any resemblance to actual persons, living or dead, or actual events is purely coincidental.

This book is sold subject to the condition that it shall not by way of trade or otherwise, be lent, resold, hired out or otherwise circulated, without the publisher's prior consent, in any form of binding or cover other than that in which it is published.

www.ukiyoto.com

CONTENTS

Smile	1
I Love You	2
Dandelion	15
The Night At Chilpata Forest	16
Decorated Imagination	20
Manchester Blast of 22nd May	23
Every Night	28
A Birthday Wish	29
"Life" – A Parabola of Enchantment	34
The Secret	36
Songbook	49
The Turning Point	51
Jessica	51
The Fairyland	53
The Beginning Of A New Life	55
The Breaking News	57
The Arrival Of The Prince	59
The Courtship	61
The Marriage	65
The Confrontation	67
The Reality	71
The Final Decision	73
Friendship is love	75
The Monk Of Tholung Gompa	77
The Invitation and the Excitement	77
The Journey	80

The Kamsil Ceremony And The Festivities	82
The Museum And Library Of Tholung Monastery	84
Dinner Time	86
The Dawn	88
The Sight of You	91
Melody Of A Piano And Scent Of Jasmine	92
Words From A Girl Called Eartha (Earth)	95
The Baptism	97
Tick Tock	104
Kiki's Cuckoo Clock	106
Voids	118
Lost	120
Sancity Of Love	122
Purpose	123
Cougar	132
Eclipse	135
The Dawn Of Enternity	158
She Is A Poetry	160
About the Authors	***162***

Smile

Vachaknavi Sarma

Your smile is an intricate
Piece of amazing Art;
Like the portrait of the Mona Lisa...
Curved like the crescent moon;
above the sea...
Like lighting a bright flame
before a face; yet to be seen...
With a bit of suspense of
what it has to prevail...
Your smile lights up lives
Like the first ray of sunshine
And brings peace to hearts
Like the moonlight...

I Love You

Johanny Ortega

Author's note: While this work is fiction, the emotions are very real. One day during the holidays my husband debated whether to live or die. That day he chose life, and he has made that choice ever since. Yet, the thought crossed my mind, 'what if...' From that morbid wandering came this story. If you or someone you know are struggling with suicide please know you are not alone. Reach out to someone.

Annotated here are only two of many services that can serve as a lifeline for those experiencing helplessness and hopelessness and wish to harm or kill themselves. U.S. Suicide Hotline number: 1-800-273-8255. The Canada Suicide Prevention Service: 1-833-456-4566.

For someone who accesses risks and finds solutions, Gabriella's mind was utterly ineffective at that moment. Her fingers went numb. The book about a sweet romance in a small town fell from her grip. She watched as her husband's hand trembled. What happened? Just a few seconds ago, she felt him move with an ease she hadn't seen in a long time. She didn't know what was in the black metal box he opened. At that exact moment she didn't want to put the book down. Yet, once she realized what was in that box, it was too late.

Metal against teeth makes a funny sound. Yet, the last thing Gabriella thought she would see on December twenty-eight would be her husband with the muzzle of his 9 mm gun stuffed between his lips. The book bounced off their bed and fell to the floor. While the sound of teeth clattering may be comical, there was nothing funny about that moment.

Gabriella scrambled for something to say. Anything. She even prayed. But felt silly because she hadn't in so long. Nevertheless, her mind searched for a magical word or phrase that would take the gun away—that would take this moment away. But the only question that came to mind was, "What are you doing?"

When nothing came from Alejandro, Gabriella rushed to his side.

An avid long-distance runner, her feet didn't know what to do within the ten feet distance between their bed and her husband with a gun. "Please," was all she could utter.

For Gabriella, those ten feet were the longest she had run.

Her husband smelled of lubricant, tequila, and desperation. Worst, he closed his eyes.

She wanted—no, she needed to see them. Perhaps if she could look into his soul, she could assess a solution and act on it, thought Gabriella. But Alejandro deprived her of this assessment. "Please," she begged again.

Her calm was evaporating, and she could feel it fluttering out of her body, second by second. "What have I done?" she asked.

This was the second empty-headed question she's asked within the span of two minutes. But at that time, Gabriella did not know. For sure, it had to be her fault, she thought.

Her mind rummaged through the list of possible sins. Constant business travel, long work hours, inattentiveness, coldness. She listed them. Nevertheless, Alejandro wouldn't open his eyes.

Suddenly, much the same way the janitor surprises her early in the morning when he turns on the lights in her office building, a light bulb turns on in her brain.

Gabriella grabbed his wrist. Don't touch the trigger, she told herself. Don't touch it. At that moment, she played with all the possible scenarios of her finger accidentally pressing the trigger. Ninety-two percent of them were fatal. The odds were not in her favor.

Unfortunately, Gabriella didn't think she could renege on the poorly thought-out solution. Alejandro may see it as a sign of giving up and would ultimately give up himself. So, knowing she'd risked it all, she pulled.

She hadn't thought of one thing: her husband's strength.

Gabriella didn't realize how weak she was until she pulled down on her husband's arm. She was wrong. Alcohol hadn't weakened his grip. His depression and tears hadn't either.

But Gabriella had her voice.

This time when she tugged, she demanded, "Look at me!"

For twenty years, she's honed her voice to command attention even in the most packed of conferences. At five foot two, she was not intimidating, but when she opened her mouth, eighty-eight percent changed their minds.

Like the others, Alejandro obeyed.

When he opened his eyes, Gabriella got lost in them.

Their bedroom was painted a cool sky blue with a teal accent wall. When they first moved in, Gabriella and Alejandro decided on a queen-sized bed for their bedroom to give each other room but not distance. Around them, there were pictures of vacations, their wedding, vow renewal. Love was interlaced in each pixel.

But not so in his eyes. It was nothing but gray walls, empty picture frames, and wilted flowers. His gaze smelled like a home that's been on the market for far too long—vacant.

A tear rolled down his cheek and landed on his neck. He blinked. The 9 mm nozzle had a sheen of saliva and snot. Gabriella refused to believe she's lost him. He was there somewhere.

"I love you so much," Gabriella heard herself say. She didn't recognize the voice, though. It was not commanding. It was soft and scared.

His lips trembled, and Gabriella listened to the clinging of teeth once again. The light-hearted sound against the loaded black steel was an oxymoron.

With the gun stuffed inside his mouth, Alejandro mumbled, "I'm so ready."

That's not him, Gabriella thought. It's not his voice. With renewed effort, Gabriella covered her husband's hand. The one holding her gun. Put her finger over his finger. The one over the trigger. She put all her weight on and pulled down on his grip.

Tomorrow is supposed to be better, she thought. It always is. Honestly, Gabriella couldn't imagine a tomorrow without him. So, when she pulled, all logical thoughts left her brain. It was only instinct and survival rushing through her brain.

Yet, she knew the worst decisions are those not thought out. The ones not analyzed to compare possible scenarios have the worst results.

The gun went off.

It was a flash of smoke and an audible pop as the bullet whizzed by Gabriella's chin right before she pulled her head away. Had she imagined it?

Her gaze followed the trajectory of the smoke and kept going. Gabriella watched in horror at the fresh hole in their bedroom ceiling right on top of her head. She hadn't imagined it. It was real.

Then a flood of thoughts crammed inside her brain. She knew exactly what she was feeling. Adrenaline. Nevertheless, the thoughts brought about a question that numbed her. Upstairs, right above them, their children slept. Had they awakened? Worst, have I killed my children?

Her stomach turned into knots. The tightest of them. And they multiplied until her entire body felt cumbersome. In her hand, she had a gun. At her feet, Alejandro wept. Gabriella's feet debated between staying or going upstairs to check on their children. But if she left him like a mutated virus, he would try again, she thought.

The house was so quiet. Too quiet. Gabriella listened for footsteps above. She heard none. She listened for the doorbell. Nothing. She listened for a knock at the door. But everything was quiet except for the sound of her husband's ragged breath and whimpers.

At that moment, Gabriella chose her husband over her children.

"I'll do anything. Please don't leave me," Gabriella begged. "I love you so much."

For four minutes, I love you so much, became her mantra. She repeated it over and over, hoping she could love him just enough for him to choose his life.

Alejandro's shoulders slumped. With his head hung, he nodded. Gabriella gasped. He was choosing life, she thought.

Immediately, Gabriella sprinted towards a box only she knew existed and hid the gun there.

When she came back, Gabriella cupped her husband's face in her hands and lifted him. He rested his back on the same vanity table he built for her five years ago. It was one of his many projects inside their home, which she cherished and used every day. The mirror attached to the maple wood table was an antique from his apartment before merging their houses and getting married twelve years ago.

Lain on top of the table was the nude lipstick she used that morning before going to work to put the final touches on a project due immediately after the holidays. When she looked up, Gabriella noted the thinning hair behind her husband's head. She hadn't noticed it before. But then she lifted her gaze and froze.

Her eyes, dark brown and red from too much blue light, looked back at her, bewildered. Like her voice, she didn't recognize this pair of eyes. Long lashes were there, now a bit sparse from the scrubbing she did, not too long ago before getting to bed. The corners had lines, reminding her of the advent of forty-five years. Whose eyes were those?

But Gabriella didn't think she could spare too much time on this thought. Alejandro was the priority this time. So Gabriella crushed her lips to her husband's and stuffed the memory of the gun, her eyes, the bullet, in another box only she knew existed.

His lips were sticky with saliva and mucus. She tasted lubricant. It was a deadly kiss.

In the space between their lips, Gabriella repeated her mantra. At one point, their knees weakened, and both fell to the floor.

She didn't know how many minutes or hours passed. But a knock at their bedroom door broke the spell of time standing still. Gabriella stood and shuffled to stand in front of her husband to cover him from view. Alejandro looked like a dead man with dead eyes and no soul, and Gabriella didn't want anyone to see him this way.

"Are you guys alright?" It was their oldest son.

Like Gabriella, her eldest son portrayed a calm exterior. His square frame glasses were slightly smudged. His gaze said, I'm panicking inside, but I don't want to let on.

"Yes, Dad is just really sad," Gabriella answered the overly complicated question with a stupidly simplified answer.

She recognized her voice now but could only imagine her face and what it showed. She didn't want to think of what she saw in the mirror and didn't want to turn around to be reminded.

"Is anyone awake?" Gabriella asked.

"No. Everyone is alright," her son replied, understanding exactly what his mom was really asking.

And no more needed to be said after that, so Gabriella nodded.

When their oldest child closed the door, Gabriella sank back down. She turned around to face her husband and once again took his face in her hands. The stubble pricked her fingers.

"I love you so much," she reminded him.

I love you so much. She repeated the mantra until the sun spilled over the horizon, splashing red, orange, and blue over the sky that not too long ago was void of stars.

Two days later, Gabriella picked up the book again. She turned to the crinkled page from when she'd thrown it on the floor and trampled over it with her foot. Gabriella placed her index finger on the last word she read that day; obsessed. Was she obsessed? With work? Achievements? So much so she'd lost sight of him? Had she driven him to misery with her obsession?

The questions flowing through her mind made her think of the smell of gun oil on her husband's lips. Her hands became numb, and Gabriella dropped the book again. This time, however, when she picked it up, it was gingerly and with reverence. She smoothed the wrinkled pages, opened her bedside drawer, placed the book inside, and closed it. She would never read that book again.

Nevertheless, when Gabriella closed the drawer, she noticed the red ring from the glass of wine she'd placed on top of it without a coaster. To think all she wanted was to unwind, Gabriella thought bitterly. But she didn't. No, not at all. She placed her palm over the ring and felt the swell from the hardened condensation over the wood. At that moment, Gabriella made a mental note to have coasters in their room.

Gabriella heard footsteps behind her and whirled so fast the room spun two more times after she turned. Her husband had stepped out of the shower and was throwing a polo over his head. There were droplets of water hanging on his hair and nape. He reached for the door.

"Where you going," she asked.

He was halfway out the door. Gabriella swung one leg over.

"To get a tool," he responded.

She swung the other leg. Then she slid her feet inside a plush pair of brown slippers. Exteriorly, she nodded. Interiorly, her heart tapped against her sternum. One step became three, and Gabriella followed her husband.

As she shadowed him, Gabriella sifted through her memory from two days ago. She remembered sprinting into the garage, placing a gun inside a box, and then blank. She shook her head at her mind's inefficiency.

Regardless, she knew it had to be there, in the garage. When Gabriella stepped into the garage, she traced the outline of each box. Inside there were many things. Holiday decorations, old Army gear her husband kept after retiring, and summer clothes they wouldn't wear for another six months. Which box? She asked herself.

When Alejandro grabbed a plier, she exhaled, and she didn't know why. Was she expecting him to find it? But the exhale was too much for Gabriella, and she became light-headed.

"I'm fixing the microwave door," said Alejandro.

He was already halfway down the hallway that connected their home to the garage. His forehead furrowed. He was looking at her as if she's grown an extra head. This caused Gabriella to look at him with the same puzzled expression he'd given her.

The light in the garage turned off from lack of movement. How long had she been standing there?

Her legs were heavy, but she moved them. The light flicked on when it noticed the motion. In what seemed like a long time, but her reasoning told her was seconds, Gabriella reached her husband's side.

He was five foot ten to her five foot two, and he looked down at her. Gabriella lost herself in his eyes. But not like two days ago. There was warmth and light there now. The honey and brown melded in his iris to make one color, and it was beautiful.

Gabriella bit the inside of her cheek. Does he not remember two days ago? "Okay, baby. I love you."

"I love you too," he said.

Still, she followed. Her steps automatically followed him. The light in the kitchen was on. The little ones sat in front of their cereal bowls. When they spotted them, they burst into screams and requests of things to do during their holiday vacation. Gabriella caught her oldest son's gaze and, with her chin, pointed at his father. He nodded, which made Gabriella feel relieved somehow.

She turned around and retraced her steps.

For what seemed like hours, Gabriella paced by every piece in her garage. A treadmill collecting dust because she prefers the road.

Five bicycles hanging on the wall, skis, snowboards, boxes, lots of them. Lots of boxes. "It has to be here," she told herself.

"What you say, honey?" Alejandro asked.

She gasped and looked up. He was standing by the door. Why did he come back? Gabriella asked herself.

Alejandro passed her. The smell of dew, forest, and earth somehow became erotic when it exuded from his pores and enveloped her. He put the plier back in one of his toolboxes.

"I love you so much," she told him.

Two years passed. Gabriella watched the blinking black dot. Her stomach turned into knots until she watched the dot move. His location was 1233 Diane Lane, their home. For just a few seconds, Gabriella took her gaze away from the road to watch the dot move from the living room to the bedroom.

"Call husband," she told her phone.

She didn't see a stop sign. As a matter of fact, Gabriella doesn't remember seeing one there before. An incoming blue truck honked while both its passenger and driver flashed the middle finger in her direction. Gabriella's breath shuddered when she let it out. She only wanted to be home, is all. A meeting ran later than she'd plan. Still, since it was the last one before the holiday break, she reasoned this will be better than holding subsequent ones over the holidays.

"Hey, baby," Alejandro replied after several rings.

His voice was animated, full of life, and that made Gabriella smile.

She observed the street to make sure there were no surprise signs ahead before Gabriella pressed FaceTime. The screen opened with his smile and warm eyes. "Hey, baby. Almost home."

"I know. I'm following you on the map."

Gabriella tilted her head back as much as she could in her car and laughed. But to her, the laughter contained a sort of nervous vibration. "I'm watching you too."

"Great minds," he replied.

"Think alike," she finished. Her eyes grew somber, and she gazed into his eyes longer than she should have. This time she didn't miss a sign but a turn. Gabriella rarely cursed, but this time she allowed for a few obscenities to cross her lips. She was in the confines of her car after all, and the children were still at school.

"I'll let you go, so you can concentrate," Alejandro said.

Gabriella shrugged her shoulders. "Apparently, I can't multitask."

"That's fine. I'll see you when you get here."

And before he pressed the end button, Gabriella blurted out. "I love you. I love you so much."

"I know. I love you too."

The screen went black. What was it? She asked herself. For a millisecond, the honey in her husband's eye disappeared. Her stomach twisted, and suddenly the four-door SUV became too small and constricting. Gabriella caressed the screen as if it were her husband's face. I love you so much, she prayed.

At 12 o'clock on a Tuesday, there was little congestion. Only the commuters that dare leave their jobs for a quick lunch were out. Everyone else was inside somewhere. So, she figured it was okay to go against the traffic signs this one time. At the sign that said 'no U-turn' Gabriella made a U-turn. She watched for a police car, but saw none. When she saw the mountains in front of her, Gabriella murmured, "There we are. Back on track."

Then she whispered her mantra, I love you so much, over and over. Her words became a song that eclipsed whatever song was playing on Hot 93.1.

And because she had several more miles to go, Gabriella opened the app again. Alejandro had not moved from their bedroom. The black dot blinked with the same rhythm that it beats underneath her ear each night before they fall to sleep.

Now, at the next street. Gabriella makes a right turn in a cul-de-sac. Every house looks the same—beige—like the sand in the desert. Then, she turns left. Gabriella knows it is her street because of the loud yellow house at the corner. She'd told Alejandro she wants their home painted a vibrant color so it can stand out. Just not an obnoxious canary yellow like their neighbors.

"I love you so much," Gabriella whispers when she sees his truck parked in front of the garage and not inside.

Gabriella turns off the car, steps out, and leaves her bags in the car. She will sort that out later, she thinks. The plants in the front drip water, but it had not rained. It hadn't rained for six months. Her phone vibrates in her pocket. She takes it out to see.

Motion in your front door, it said.

"No, shit." Gabriella curses for the second time today.

Her hands shake when she inserts the key. She doesn't know why. They just do. Before she can get the key inside they fall in a puddle of water next to their lemon plant.

"Ugh," Gabriella complains.

She bends over to pick it up.

She smells lemon.

A shot rings from inside.

Gabriella jerks upright. Her hand trembles uncontrollably as she inserts the key.

All the while, she prays:

I love you so much.

I love you so much.

I love you so much.

Dandelion

Vachaknavi Sarma

You kissed my soul
With dandelion poetry...
With calm moonlight
In your eyes...
And bright warm sunshine
In your smile...
Untamed wolf in your breath
Touching even the untouched
Corners of my heart ;
Sweet and wild...

The Night At Chilpata Forest

Dipannita Bhattacherya

I was looking at the ceiling fan of my room. It was rotating full speed, with an eerie screeching sound. I woke up from deep sleep feeling cold. The sound of the fan was annoying too. Definitely, I didn't switch it on when I slept as I didn't need it then. October nights in Dooars are pretty cool and comfortable.

The Dooars region, at the foothills of the Eastern Himalayas, has some enchanting Reserved Forests, Wildlife Sanctuaries, and National Parks. I have been frequenting these forests for many years now. Yet, I haven't been able to visit Chilapata Forests in Dooars in the last five years. Chilapata is near the famous Jaldapara National Park of Dooars. My job entails traveling to Indian forests regularly. Chilapata was notorious for poachers and dacoits, to such an extent, that for the last three years even the government could not operate here. Recently, the new government seems to have brought about some peace and security measures for officers like us to work here safely.

Let's get back to the ceiling fan. I switched off the winding fan, pulled the light blanket over my face, and went back to sleep.

The screeching sound was maddening even in my sleep. I woke up again. The room appeared darker this time or maybe my sleep had been deeper. The fan was switched on again. "Something is wrong with the switches," I thought as I reached for the bed switch and found that it was not working.

I was hurriedly getting up from my bed to switch the fan off when I realized that there was someone in the room. I sat still, not even moving my little finger. I felt heavy. I couldn't breathe. I could see a silhouette of a thin, tall man at the door. The silhouette's hair seemed disheveled and frizzy. Surely I had bolted the door from inside. I never make such a not-so-silly mistake. I wanted to shout but not a sound escaped my throat.

"Babu, your door was not locked from inside. I am sorry I came in without permission. I had knocked but you seemed to be sleeping. I came inside to get you out of the room." said a husky rural voice.

"Who are you? I will call the guards," I said with a trembling voice.

"Please come out with me. I am Mungla, the old caretaker, if you remember. I remember you. You are a good man. You praised my cooking and had generously tipped me in your last visit, five years ago. You have to leave this room now," said Mungla as he held my wrist to drag me out of the bed at lightning speed.

His touch was ice cold. We left the room.

Outside the room, there was a dimly lit lantern. I could hardly see Mungla's face but I could recognize him. I remember the fact that he has magic fingers when it comes to cooking.

"What does all this mean Mungla?" I questioned angrily. He walked towards the lawn without answering and I followed anxiously.

Mungla started, "Babu, do you remember the incident of Parbat Torai?" I replied, "Yes, Parbat Torai was the deadliest poacher of Chilapata Forest. He was caught five years ago and his gang obnoxiously killed forest officers for revenge. Even the government had to stop core operations here for the last two or three years."

"Parbat believed no one could ever catch him. He had managed to escape repeatedly before. His four-year-old son was used as bait by the government officers this time. So he finally had to surrender. They left him and his little son tied up in that room, where you were sleeping tonight. Parbat knew of the officers' plan to shoot him in encounter behind closed door. He managed to cut open the ropes but was unable to escape. He first hung his little son to death and then himself. They hung from that ceiling fan of your room," Mungla's voice trembled as he narrated the horrifying story. "I was the one who opened the door first and found their dead bodies. Parbat's curse prevails in that room, in that fan."

The moment I tried to picture what Mungla said, I felt like vomiting. Yet, I firmly exclaimed, "Superstitions!! There's nothing called a curse. What happened with the little child is unfortunate. That was not desired, I am sure. Parvat was a notorious poacher who deserved punishment. His gang killed the ranger and the other officers from his team in the same fashion, for revenge."

"Yes, they hung one by one, from the same fan of the same room. It was because of the curse. However, Parvat's gang didn't do a thing. They had fled from Chilapata after the news of Parvat's unpleasant death. You urban chaps don't believe us, the uneducated people of the jungle. But we know the truth. The officers shouldn't have used his little son. None was spared. Even I was not," Mungla said regretfully.

I was about to say something to him when I was interrupted by a sudden crashing sound that seemed to have come from my room. I headed towards my room hurriedly without noticing if Mungla came along. The guards came running too.

"Where were you two? Why are no lights on?" I questioned the guards strictly. One of the two replied, "Sorry Sir, we were playing cards. Electricity supply issues are common here. The generator is not yet repaired." I snapped, "Electricity issue? My fan was on inside my room."

I opened the door and shockingly found the old and heavy ceiling fan fell on my crumbled bed. "O God, I would have been gravely injured, it could have been fatal. Did Mungla actually save me?" I said to myself. Frantically I started looking for Mungla calling out his name loudly, "Mungla? Mungla? Where did you go?" Then I ordered the guards, "One of you please get Mungla here. He is at the lawn."

The bewildered guard replied, "Sir, did you just call Mungla? This fan had similarly fallen from the ceiling on his head when he was cleaning the room. Mungla died two years ago."

Decorated Imagination

Vachaknavi Sarma

You have no idea
how happy I am to be in love with you.
I want to scream from my lungs till I'm breathless and blue.
I want the world to know how excited I am
To finally be in love.. with this gorgeous,
fabulous, and perfect man.

How lucky I am; it feels like a
crazy hullabaloo inside.
It feels like I'm riding this big
roller coaster of pride.
My mind is always bombarded
with numerous thoughts of you.
Is this the beginning of something new?
Or I'm just going crazy??
I swear a single thought of you makes

my mind hazy...
How smitten I am with those eyes of black or maybe brown.
That runs through my mind and heart and
takes away my frown.
And your mesmerizingly calming smile,
makes me weak at the knees,
Sweeps me off my feet like a powerful breeze.

I decorate my imagination with roses and wine,
a candle or two.
Those tiny stars shine brighter for you and me.

How ecstatic I am; my heart races and thumps.
Thinking of you, I get little goosebumps.
You're affectionate, ambitious, alluring, caring, intimidating, funny, and smart,
Definitely molded into a very fine piece of art.

How my emotions have taken over me,
And suddenly life's better completely, you see.
You are one in a million; I have to be true.
I am now understanding the magic of you.

Honey, your heart I promise keep warm and protect,
For I value you with the utmost respect.
I hope my love for you will always remain

selfless magical and new,
Because nowhere on this entire universe
I'll find a man one-tenth the likes of you...

Manchester Blast of 22nd May

Vachaknavi Sarma

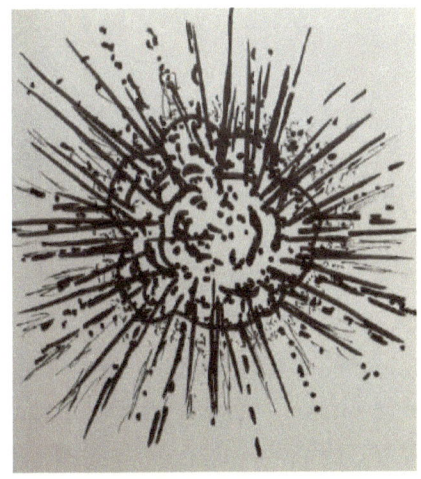

It was about 10 pm, we were at a nearby cafe. We were still debating on why I and Andrew decided to ditch the Grande concert even after having the tickets. And Nessa was being picked on for being a lazy bum.

The cafe was so full of life. We could even hear Ariana's gigs from there.

Katie said, "What a waste! We have the tickets right here! And what are we doing? Sitting our asses here waiting to eat sandwiches!! F**k you girls... You people are so lethargic!"

"I know right! We were dressed up and ready. But these two and Andy messed it all up!", Added Emily.

Andrew got up to go place an order and said, "Keep bitching ladies! I'm off to place our order!"

"Get me a soda popsicle as well please" Added Nessa.

I said, "We were tired Em, Kate! Besides I told ya we'd watch it on the television!! You didn't agree!"

Nessa added, "Hell yeah! Wouldn't have made much of a difference! Would it??"

Kate and Emily replied after looking at each other, smiled "Actually not. But we could've saved money on these tickets. Right!" We nodded in agreement.

Andrew came to the table, took a seat and said, "Sorry ladies, it's gonna take a hell lotta time. The place is packed!" And he added looking at me, "Sorry Boo there's no chocolate milkshake. So I ordered cold coffee for you. That's okay I guess!"

I replied "Umm-hmm!"

Andrew looked at his watch and said, "It's about 10:20, and food must be ready in 30!"

And we got busy in our debate about how good it'd be inside the Arena and how comfortable our couch would be. And in a few minutes, the gig had ended. And we could hear people hooting and shouting with happiness for it was an awesome evening.

"Awwww, we missed such a good show. Man, I wish we went!" Emily blurted all of a sudden. We all added in unison, "Awwwwwww!", and shared a good laugh. Just then Andrew added seeing a woman come out followed by a bunch of more people, "Hah! They are out, Ariana's show was great."

.............and BOOOOM, all I can remember is we laid our head on the table covering it with our hands. And when I raised my head all I could see people running in terror, a few covered in blood, some people on the floor shouting and yelping in pain. Metal pieces everywhere, smog from the blast and pieces of shrapnel and glass.

Tears rolled down my cheeks and I didn't even know why! My ears felt numb for a moment from the big boom noise. I rubbed my ears for a bit and wiped my tears.

And then Kate patted me on my shoulder and said with a terrified voice, "Come on Boo, we need to go help people... They need me (she's an NHS employee)... They need us.

All of us. Get a grip. We... Help... Them... Whatever possible! Get up Boo, if we need to drive them to the hospitals. It's only you and Andrew who can. Come on!!"

We all rushed across the street and started helping the police to help the people and helped the 'walking injured' reach the hospitals or the nearby medic providing medication.

And then I saw a few of my colleagues hurt, some severely injured... I ran up to them and the view I saw made me scream, "OUCH! Are they... What can... Should... Help... How?? Tell me!!! PLEASE!!!"

One of those who were a little less injured told, "Ma'am, calm down, you are in a traumatic shock.. So are we. You will need to stop crying and ask one of those medics to come up here. Can you?" I nodded and ran to a nearby medic and said with folded hands, "My friends... Bleeding... Too bad... Help... Please. I dunno what else.."

He stopped me midway, hugged me, and said, "Honey it's okay, please relax, we're here. We'll help your friends. They'll be fine. Trust me we're here to help. Come... Take me to them. But first, lemme see if you are hurt."

I replied pointing to the cafe, "No... I was... There... Not hurt.."

He replied, "Oh Hun! Lemme see; you were only 4 or 5 meters away!"

He checked on me and said, "You are fine... Physically... Now let's go check on those friends of yours!"

We reached where my severely injured colleagues were and the medic checked on them and said on his walkie, "Type 4, severe injury, inside of the gate, bring in 7 gurneys... Right now... ASAP!"

And right in a few moments, more medics arrived with gurneys and one by one put the injured on those gurneys on count of threes.

In the hospital, the scenes were more horrific. Katie started helping doctors with minor surgeries. Vanessa and Emily helped with the unattended children there. Andrew was driving people from the

Arena to the hospitals. I was there at St. Mary's hospital. I could see people moving around me shouting for help, crying in terror and pain. I could see doctors going from patient to patient, changing blood-stained gloves each time. I swear I could see everything happen in slow motion. And could hear each cry for help loud and clear. I looked around and around and around.

And suddenly I sat down on the floor grabbing my ears and shouted at the top of my voice, " Nooooooooo!!" A doctor and Em rushed to me.. Em hugged me and said, "It's okay Boo... We are all okay... Boo... Get up... You can't break down this way... This is the first for all of us... And you are the bravest Boo. And I'm glad we didn't go to the concert."

She then turned to the doctor and said, "She's okay... Just a bit traumatized."

The doc said, "You are all suffering from Post Traumatic Stress. You'll get over it... And thank you so much for helping us out. We're grateful." He then cupped my cheek, planted a soft kiss, and said, "You are a strong young lady... You've been through a lot... And this night is getting harder... For all of us... Stay strong... Your friends there in the critical care would need you. Right??" And he walked away to check on the injured patients.

I grabbed control over myself and went out to help Andrew drive people from the Arena to hospitals.

The night of 22/5/17 was a real long one.

 It had yet not ended. By Tuesday (the next day) late morning, I lost a friend who was critically injured in the blast.

And on the same evening, one of our friends drove a long way to find his school-going sister who was missing ever since the blast. After searching for her in every hospital and looking at each unnamed injured, our search ended at a mortuary. A little child had lost her life.

In the following early morning, the news of one of my colleagues plus friend becoming an angel came to me.

The pain and the terror have marked themselves on my soul with permanent ink.

These memories will never leave me.. However bad I want them to go. My heart has been bleeding ever since Monday 10:30 PM.

I can't yet believe what I've seen and what we've been through. What Manchester had been through.

So many kids were lost. So many still missing. I have no idea what my friends and families are going through.

I can't even express what I'm going through. I can't express my pain and horror in words...

I feel being an eyewitness is a curse. And a bigger one if your memory becomes photographic. Every moment right from the blast till now floats across my eyes as soon as I close them. And I sit up in terror with tears rolling down my eyes.

It was such a pleasant evening which turned into a horrendous night.

P. S.: This time it's real... Not a work of my imagination.

Every Night

James Kinsella

Under the moonlight, I write my poems
Amongst the evening stars, faint glows
Daily journeys when writing these prose
Spellbound feelings create these poems

Amid the summer roses, aromatic smells
A thousand memories whisper to my pen
Dripping ink dreams create those poetic bells
The poet in me bloomed, once again

A Birthday Wish

Kuntala Bhattacharya

Jhelum was born in a rich family, a family where she never missed any moment of luxury. She had all the grandeur of a palace and all the amenities at her fingertips.

You must be thinking that her parents would have treated her like a princess in a kingdom. But that was the only irony of her life. She hardly got a cuddle from her parents, being awkwardly tendered only by her nannies. Little did she knew about the bonding between parents and a child.

Jhelum's father was one of the richest businessmen of the town and seldom invested time for his family. His main commitment to the family was the frequent lavish parties and the attendance of his peers in business. Well, he of course never forgot to bring expensive gifts for his wife and daughter. But the gifts were brought only to show the power of money and not the power of love.

Jhelum's mother remained engrossed with herself and the kitty parties with her lady friends most of the time. She liked boasting about her jewelry and the numerous expensive dresses she possessed. The ladies loved to engage themselves in discussing about their luxurious belongings.

Jhelum's parents never bothered to celebrate birthdays; they seldom wanted to be accompanied by their daughter. She used to envy her friends celebrating and inviting her to their birthday parties. Though she pretended to enjoy with her friends at the parties, yet deep down she had a pain engraved inside her heart. A pain that was irreparable and inconsolable.

Soon Jhelum grew up to be a young lady and started her college days. She had always been selective in choosing her friends. Her loneliness at home acted as a hindrance in being social and cordial with others of her age.

Raj was one of the students in her class. He came from a mediocre family but was a scholar student merited with intelligence and smartness. His parents had taught him discipline, the value of life, how to love and share with others, and celebrating small happiness of life. He had an incredible power of being friendly with all his classmates. Soon he observed Jhelum being mostly silent in any friendly discussions or gossips in the class or even within the college campus.

One fine day during the recess, he approached Jhelum in the college canteen. Jhelum was sitting alone at a table in the corner and was munching her packed lunch from home. Her only friend in the class, Anu, was absent and so she had none to speak with.

The moment she observed Raj approaching her table, she became conscious. Her uneasiness was quite observable.

"Hey Jhelum, can I join you for lunch?" Raj stood near the table with a smiling face.

Jhelum's face instantly turned red. With confusion creeping her all over, she managed to answer, "Yes please".

"Thank you," Raj uttered and sat down at the chair beside her.

"I know I have intruded into your silent world. But we study in the same class and thought why not be friends", Raj tried to ease out the situation with a light conversation.

"No no, it's perfectly fine. My bestie Anu is absent today and I am very shy in mingling with people. So was just sitting here alone with my lunch," Jhelum answered with hesitation apparent in her voice.

"So, where do you stay? My house is nearby. I mostly come walking or on my bike," Raj started with a regular question.

"My house is about 30 minutes from here. I come by car. The driver drops me here every day. That's how it is," a smile blushed across Jhelum's face as she answered Raj's question.

Raj noticed that she was amazingly beautiful yet very shy and conservative in her conversations. "Wow, you are a privileged girl. I hope I can buy a car once I get a decent job", giggled Raj.

"Actually, on the contrary, I like walking and cycling. Traveling constantly in the car is sometimes boring and monotonous", sighed Jhelum.

"Hmm, gotcha! Well if you agree to be friends with me, then I can surely walk you sometimes to school or home. What say? Are you in for that?" Raj enquired with a gracious smile on his face.

"Oh, that's so nice of you. Sure we can be friends. I have so few people to speak to in college," Jhelum's face sparkled with happiness. She felt grateful. Never in her life has someone approached her to accept her as a friend.

"Well then, there are some ground rules to agree on in our friendship. Are you ready to hear that, Jhelum?" Raj demanded.

"Oops rules, Okay! Yes sure, what are those?" Jhelum was taken by surprise. Friendship, for her, was such an unknown concept. She could never think of rules into it. Raj quite amused her. An inner voice seemed to coax her to know him more.

"It's simple but tough too. We share every bit and piece of our daily life and even past life. It can be bad or good. But we share and discuss. We may land up in arguments and fights. Yet we never keep any secrets. Do you agree? I will do the same too," Raj spoke out.

After few seconds of silence, Jhelum replied, "Yes I agree and I will do the same".

That's it. From that day, a strong friendship developed between the two. They were inseparable. Discussing, debating, fighting, and then reconciling. All were a part of their lives. In college, others started envying them. They even teased them to be couples. But they ignored all such rumours. Their bonding strengthened day by day.

Jhelum learned a lot from Raj. Social life for her was an unknown creature. Raj told her about human values and how precious relations are.

Jhelum used to listen to him for hours, completely engrossed in the conversations.

One fine day Raj asked her, "When is your birthday?" Jhelum was like, "What? Why is that important?"

Raj was completely taken by surprise, "Are you crazy? Birthday is the most important day of one's life. Don't your parents celebrate your birthday? They must be wishing you on your birthday".

Jhelum was unable to believe Raj's words. Sadly she said, "No they never celebrated my birthday and never wished me." She had seen movies where they show birthday parties and how she wished she had the same. But she had started believing parties happen only in movies or dreams and not in reality. Raj's words brought her thoughts back and engulfed her in a world of sadness. Unable to control herself she suddenly started crying.

Raj got worried, he immediately held her and comforted her.

"What's wrong Jhelum? Why are you crying? Are you upset because your parents never celebrated your birthday? I think I made you sad today. I am so sorry, Jhelum".

Jhelum, enfolding herself within the comforting hands of Raj, uttered emotionally, "No Raj, how can you hurt me? You are my best friend with whom I can share everything, my sorrows, my joys. I never knew how birthdays are precious. I am crying because today is my birthday."

An elegant smile flourished across Raj's face. He lifted the moist face of Jhelum and looked into her eyes. "Hey Jhelum, no crying now. We are going to celebrate this day in such a grand fashion that all your tears will vanish and happiness will embrace you."

Jhelum suddenly felt awkward. "No Raj please, no parties. I am not used to such celebrations. Let's forget it and go for some coffee", said Jhelum wiping off her tears.

Raj gave a wink and asked Jhelum to follow him and trust him. He made some quick phone calls which Jhelum could not guess. They took a cab and stopped in front of a small restaurant in the middle of an eco-village. Jhelum had never been to this place. The place had a simplistic view with greenery all around and the chirping of birds here and there. There was a small pool of water beside the restaurant. Raj summoned Jhelum to follow him towards the pool where they could sit.

Suddenly, the air started ringing up in light music. Raj stood up and took up a guitar. "Happy Birthday to you. Happy Birthday to you. Happy Birthday dear Jhelum. Happy Birthday to you".

Tears rolled down Jhelum's cheeks and a delightful smile beautified her face. With a lovely twinkle in her eyes, she tugged herself into Raj's shirt. Raj spread his hands to embrace her.

That day they decided to be partners for life.

"Life" – A Parabola of Enchantment

Kuntala Bhattacharya

Life is a parabola of joyous enchantment
You spin it and it rebounds in merriment
Deciphering monumental happiness in its core
Scouting into instances of galore.

Life is infused with infinite excitement
Percolating morality from sinful indictment
Traversing high and low wrapped in dreams
Bountifully revitalizing for a rise to the supreme.

Life is an envelope of immense exhilaration
Fulfilling aspirations into realistic ambition
Unearthing the riddle concealed within it

Intensifying the enormous mystery dwelling in it.

Life is a storehouse of passions and desires
Plunging deep inside into its circle of fancies
Engrossing the heart and mind in its melancholy
Proliferating dreams into monumental glory.

Life is a plethora of elation and enthusiasm
Bouncing and blooming into its charming blossom
Drenching the soul within an enigmatic aura
Hypnotizing oneself into its appealing flora.

Life is a gift of God, the Almighty of this Universe
Nourishing every single bit to keep it illustrious
Enriching the marvel camouflaged by its gracious dignity
Refining and polishing the colossal creativity.

Life is a stage of dramatic vivacity
Embellishing with its warmth and generosity
Comforting the core with kindliness and geniality
Adoring and nurturing to the divine eternity.

The Secret

Sanjana Chhatlani

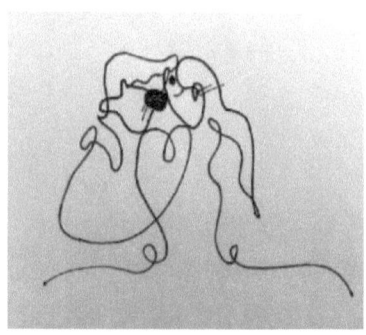

Kritika felt all muddled and shaky as she groggily opened her eyes. Every muscle she could feel in her body was screaming and aching as if asking for some kind of release. She could barely keep her eyes open for a few seconds, blinking rapidly, but the weight on the eyelids seemed too overbearing and she gave in quickly, shutting them back.

She tried to make sense of her surroundings. Everything around was too quiet. Flashes of past events began to come alive before her eyes.

The fear, the stealth, the money, the bags, the bus, Anand... Anand?

She panicked and opened her eyes, frantically looking around. There were all sorts of tubes and wires jutting out of her body.

She finally remembered the entire sequence of events. They had met with an accident. The bus they were traveling in...

She panicked even more and started screaming for Anand, but her vocal cords wouldn't lend any support. She tried harder and harder, desperately trying to get a grip over herself. Before she knew it, a nurse, a doctor, her parents, and her younger sister, all gathered around her. It was like waking up into a dead world, a nightmare! She couldn't hear anything anyone said.

She dug her fingers into her ears in an attempt to shake herself out of the silent trance that encaged her and seemingly threatened her existence. But to no avail. She tried to speak, but couldn't hear her voice. She screamed and screamed. Everyone felt distraught to hear her, which meant she did have a voice, but she couldn't hear it. Slowly, after a futile battle against the inevitable, she sunk into acceptance in a flood of tears and her mother's warm hug. She had lost the ability to hear.

Nothing would ever be the same again. In the next month that she continued to stay in the hospital, she recuperated from most of the other injuries and fractures. A sign language teacher helped her and the family to communicate. In time she was able to manage fairly well with the basics. Then there was always written communication for the more complicated conversations.

Bouts of aggression, denial, and depression marred her recovery. A counselor was assigned to help her cope with the situation. But she had shut herself into a world of non-communication. She refused to delve into that past, divulge any details or allow anyone to heal her. Because she knew nothing could. Her family would never know what had happened, neither would they understand.

She belonged to a conservative but highly educated and well-to-do family. Just a few months back, when all was hunky-dory, she had made innumerable attempts to convince her family to meet Anand. She told them they loved each other and she wanted to marry him.

According to them, he was a complete misfit, due to inferiority in caste, class, and culture. Let alone meet, they refused to even continue a conversation in that direction, shutting all possible doors on her, leaving her with no choice but to elope with her beloved.

But fate had destined otherwise. The bus they took to another State that night, fell into a gorge, killing many and grievously injuring the others. A rescue team got her admitted to the hospital and her parents were informed. Immediately after regaining consciousness, she had to come to terms with being deaf and therefore also dumb.

All her initial concern and anxiousness for Anand vanished. She decided she would not attempt to even find out anything about Anand. What was the point anyway? If he was dead, she didn't want to know and if he was alive, she didn't want to meet him. Broken and incomplete, she didn't want to be a part of his life anymore. Besides, if he was alive, her parents could make things difficult for him, frame a case on him, or do something even more ghastly. And she would probably not be in a position to defend him. She decided; everything that she had dreamt and lived for in the past 4 years was just over.

That one night had turned her world upside down, shattered her dreams, and robbed her of the will to live.

Ironically, her parents wanted to talk and know more. About him, about their plans, about that night… but they only met with a cold, faraway gaze. She had broomed all her emotions behind layers of bitterness and angst that refused to find expression. In turn, it kept eating her from within, increasing bouts of sickness.

Her friends made various attempts to meet her. She refused and shunned away from social media completely, deleting all her accounts on various handles. She gave up her mobile too.

Her parents tried to persuade her to stay communicable via messages, but she had made up her mind. Her friends sent letters, but she never opened them or read them. They forced themselves into her house to meet her but she shut herself in her room. She didn't want to see her helplessness and inferiority in their eyes. Neither did she want their sympathy. After a year, they slowly gave up.

She did feel curious about Anand at various times, itching to know if he had survived, if he was ok. But she killed any curiosity that arose, for the fear that it could send wrong signals and fuel a keenness to get together. She had resigned to her fate, but even so, it had to be on her terms.

She confined herself to the house, refusing to even step out. The absence of music, happy chattering with friends, long conversations with Anand on the phone, his pranks, and the absence of the general din and bustle of everyday life, the ringing of the bell, the chirping of the birds, the noise of the vehicles, mom's morning prayers; everything seemed to have gone on mute and all that silence pushed her deeper and deeper into darkness and depression. A sordid, dull, and lifeless persona replaced the gregarious, fun-loving Kritika.

Her parents then decided to continue her education with a special tutor to keep her occupied and give her purpose. She carried on mechanically without any life and soul, like a robot, programmed to do certain tasks every day. The only happy time she had during the day was when she drowned herself in happy memories of the past.

She often reminisced about the day she first met Anand and how they fell in love. The sweet nothings, the fun and adventure in meeting up away from the prying eyes of the world, the amazing fact that they hadn't fought even a single day in the four years of their courtship, it would all fill her with joy momentarily and then depress her. But she clung to those memories like a hidden treasure that no one could take away from her.

Sometimes she would remember specific incidents that had become the highlight of their journey together. Prankster that he was, on one occasion, Anand had put up a fake notice on the noticeboard about an upcoming fancy dress competition. Kritika had taken it seriously and on his suggestion, donned the get-up of a tribal woman, complete with accessories like the straw basket, the heavy metal jewelry, and a whole bouquet of flowers in her head. Much to her embarrassment, the whole college had laughed. She could only hide her face in her hands with embarrassment and then beat Anand to a pulp with that very basket, while he couldn't stop laughing. He had then sheepishly announced that he wanted to see her in tribal attire and she had melted!

On another occasion, when the results for the year were declared, he made a forlorn face and told her he had flunked. That broke her heart. Since she was very studious, she felt so tense and upset that she couldn't stop crying. But Anand had laughed his head off seeing her cry, and disclosed his lie. She remembered running after him to thrash him all over college. She'd always catch him and spank him in jest. Those were fun and happy days. Those memories always brought innumerable smiles but also left her in tears. She lived and relived those days every day.

Three months later, one day, Ramona, a common friend dropped by and made earnest requests to meet her. After multiple requests,

Kritika finally relented but met Ramona alone in her room. Ramona told her that Anand had survived the accident too and had been desperately trying to meet her. Kritika cut her off mid-way and categorically told her to tell Anand to forget about her, and that she was not interested, and that it had all been a big mistake. Having said that, she refused to let Ramona even say anything further on the topic. She even made Ramona promise her that she wouldn't ever try and be a messenger for Anand again. Neither would Ramona give Anand any feedback or information about her ever again after this day. Days and months passed with increasing drudgery of existence and gloom.

Kritika's parents were consumed with guilt, seeing their child so miserable. They made various attempts to talk to her about Anand. But she had built a fortress around her memories and she kept them securely guarded in the vault of her heart. She allowed no one inside.

Four more years passed by, living each day like a punishment. She finally managed to complete her education and her parents coaxed her to take up a job with a company that hired differently-abled people and helps them lead a life of dignity. She had been brilliant with academics, so landing the job wouldn't be tough. But she refused. She didn't want human interaction. She had made isolation her way of life. They were worried sick about her.

Finally one day her dad came up to her with tears in his eyes and said, 'Kritika, you will have to get over the past. You can't keep punishing yourself when there have been mistakes on both sides. We were wrong to not listen to you when you approached us. There is a life ahead of you. We won't be here all your life to take care of you. If you get married and settle down, the thought that you have a family by your side will at least let us die in peace. We just can't leave you at the mercy of the world, with no support system in place. I need to make you secure. Please think about it. There are special bureaus that help specially-abled people find their partners.'

That night Kritika cried herself to sleep. She had given up the thought of settling down in life ever, but she realized that slowly she would become a burden on her parents too. Anger and grief repeatedly surfaced despite her best attempts to come to terms with the situation.

After mulling over it for a month, and with repeated persuasion from her parents, she finally relented. The parents registered her on various matrimonial sites for finding her a suitable alliance. They also spread the word in the community that they were looking for a suitor for their daughter. It broke their heart to look for specially-abled boys, but it was a reality they had to accept too.

Two more months later, her father finally came up with a list of seven boys from the matrimonial site whom the parents felt, best suited her. He told her to go through the bio-data of each one and then decide whom she'd like to meet. With a heavy heart, she began to look at the short-listed candidates.

One had lost a leg, another one was just like her. Their personal information seemed relatively impressive as they had achieved a lot even after facing a limitation. This time caste, creed, culture, status, nothing mattered. The focus was only on finding an understanding and caring life partner.

She looked at their photographs. She couldn't relate to anyone. They were strangers and she was not inclined to meet them or know them. And how could she possibly spend the rest of her life with someone she'd meet a couple of times maybe. The thought choked her. Disheartened, she flipped through the remaining photographs without even reading their details. Then she logged out of her account on the website and scrolled through random other boys absent-mindedly.

Suddenly, among the boys, she saw the photograph of Anand staring back at her. Anand? Her heart skipped a beat. What was he doing on that site? It was meant for people with impairments only. With trembling hands, she clicked on the link to his bio-data. He had lost his vision. Her head reeled and her body shook violently. The world around collapsed. She had come to terms with the fact that he was fine and that he would eventually settle down in his own life. The thought never even crossed her mind that he could have faced a similar fate too.

Ramona had come to speak about him. But she had never mentioned impaired vision. Kritika remembered not even allowing Ramona to talk. Tears streamed down her face. She had accepted all that had happened to her, but his disability was too much for her to absorb. For the first time, there was an avalanche of anger in her. She turned violent and began to throw things and howl. Her parents came running into the room.

She couldn't stand their sight. They were responsible for all that she had been through but she had taken it all. She had reconciled to the thought that her karma had brought this suffering upon her. The thought of Anand turning blind because of all this was unacceptable. A huge struggle ensued, and her father was finally able to hold her firmly as she slumped, crying. They couldn't understand what had gotten over her.

Kritika requested to meet Ramona after nearly four and a half years. Ramona agreed and met her two days later. Kritika couldn't stop herself and cried inconsolably as she pointed out Anand's photograph on the matrimonial site and questioned her. Ramona then told her that she had come to tell her the same thing but Kritika hadn't even allowed her to speak then. Anand had indeed lost his vision in the accident. He was registered on the site by the name of Vijayanand, his complete name, but everyone addressed him as Anand.

Kritika felt miserable to think he was going through such a tough phase in his life because of her and she had been so nasty. She decided she wouldn't tell her parents anything initially and expressed her desire to meet him. Her parents were surprised she had chosen to meet a blind boy. How would they even communicate? He wouldn't be able to see what she said in gestures and she wouldn't be able to hear him when he spoke. It was normal for a person with impaired hearing to select someone with a similar condition as they would understand and communicate with each other perfectly. Or even choose someone with a physical limitation. But this kind of alliance was tremendously challenging and next to impossible.

When they went to his house to meet him, she took Ramona along. Anand came into the room, black glasses on his eyes, groping with his stick. Face to face with him for the first time since the accident and seeing him in that state, tears streamed down her face. No one mattered. She became oblivious to the world around her. She ran to him and hugged him.

Her parents were shocked! When she revealed, he was Anand, her long-lost love with whom she had eloped, everyone fell silent. Strange are the ways of destiny. Watching the two broken souls get back together after going through so much left everyone speechless!

Deeply saddened that the tragic state of the two children was because of him, her father collapsed. He had refused to meet the boy or even reason out with his daughter years ago. Had he taken a different approach then, the two could have been together without being incapacitated like this. No matter how sorry he felt, the damage couldn't be undone. Karma can play crazy games. He couldn't undo the past, but he could repair the future. The two had to be together. There was no other way. Destiny wouldn't bring them together twice without reason. They were meant to be.

So he decided he would do whatever it took to restore Anand's eyesight, even if it meant an eye transplant. He had tried various treatments to restore his daughter's hearing ability, but so far it had been in vain. While he would continue to find a solution for her, Anand mentioned the doctors saying that his eyesight could be restored. Since his problem had a sure-shot cure, Kritika's father decided he would do everything in his capacity, financial or otherwise, to ensure Anand can see again.

Meanwhile, even with all their limitations, Kritika and Anand's joy knew no bounds. After years, there was so much happiness and love in the air. But Kritika expressed her desire to communicate with Anand first. Everyone wondered how they could get the two to talk to each other... Ramona came up with an easy solution. She downloaded an App for Kritika which would voice everything she typed so Anand could hear it. Then she downloaded another App for Anand that would type out whatever he said, so Kritika could read.

Kritika began with,' I love you' and Anand responded with 'I love you too' amid cheers and laughter from everyone around. Kritika then wrote,

'Anand, in due course, your eyesight will be restored. Then will you still want to spend the rest of your life with me? I may not recover. Life will be tough.'

Kritika's father understood what his daughter said and also understood the humungous difficulty they would face if they came together. But he made up his mind and spoke to her in sign language. He said there was no turning back. Both of them couldn't do without each other. Life had given them a second chance and there was no other way. They were destined to be together.

Anand too replied saying, 'Kritika, if you feel that we can be equals only until my vision is impaired then so be it. I won't go for treatment. But I choose to be with you always.'

Kritika shuddered and wrote, 'No, that is not what I meant. I..'

Her father intervened. 'That's it then. No more dwelling on this. I took your happiness away once. I wouldn't do it by any means again. Don't you see? This is how it was meant to be. Why be pessimistic and give up on your treatment? Miracles keep happening. There are constant technological advancements. What if you can hear in the future? Wouldn't you regret it then if you let Anand go now?'

Kritika thought for a while and then nodded in acceptance. There was another round of cheering. Everyone jumped into celebration mode. Sweets were exchanged and a wedding date was decided.

Then suddenly, Anand removed the dark glasses before his eyes and said,

'Now that everything is settled, I have a confession to make. I can see.'

Everyone gasped! Kritika looked at him in disbelief!.

He continued, 'I did lose my eyesight in the accident, but I went through an eye transplant 10 months back. My eyesight is already restored. I knew though, that if the fact was disclosed earlier, Kritika would refuse to even meet me. Ramona had revealed everything about Kritika's unwillingness to even speak to me ever again. I just want to tell Kritika that losing my eyesight, then being in that state for more than three years, and finally getting my vision back has only made me more empathetic as a person towards life, people, and circumstances. This is not a decision taken out of sympathy, though. It is only out of love. I could have chosen to stay away had I wanted to. But I can't. I don't want to have a life without you. I will be an understanding husband because I have been through it. I know what it means and what it takes to be in that state. Word had spread that you were looking for a groom. I put up my bio-data on every single matrimonial site for the differently-abled and also approached all the local bureaus. I knew when she would see that I was blind, she would approach me. But if I approached her first, she wouldn't even consider it. So I set things up. If she hadn't noticed me on the website; I had planned to make a bureau approach her casually with my bio-data among some others. And I can vehemently say that I know Kritika inside-out. Wasn't I right?'

Everyone listened in shock but also with awe and admiration. Kritika's happiness doubled. With those guilt pangs off her chest, she decided to look forward positively.

Kritika's father felt humbled. What a blunder he had made! One could never judge a person only based on background, caste, class, etc. Anand was a gem of a person and perfect for his daughter. He was happy!

Ramona happily hugged both of them and then said,

'On a lighter note, remember that Kritika is not going to listen to you, so you will always have to find a roundabout way to get her to listen to you.'

Everyone laughed. 'Well, I will be one lucky person to have a wife who talks less' Anand said merrily and they all laughed again.

Songbook

James Kinsella

Prologue

From the beginning to the end
A love story inscribed in a songbook
That's where this lifecycle was recorded
In a songbook created from memories
Vows expressed in wedding rings

A songbook of love garbed in romance
As songbirds open each verse with a sigh
Taking a moment to breathe in the love
Written in golden ink bound in precious words

Each page gently turned to unveil the verses
A vision to the mind, charming to the eyes
Old memories carried as reminders for two
Of pleasant times together when being two

These tunes transcend the bridge of time
Each note symbol in a heart shape on each sheet
Expressing a love story in tunes arise in feelings
Inscribed on these golden pages array in romance

Over the years, this book grew as like love
Happening years ago to preserve those memories
Dry flatten flowers bookmark memorable pages
Old eyes now view these old songs as sung

A book of songs written in heart shape symbols
Tune notes that were cherished and to be sung
A recollection of two woven hearts
In their embarkment on love
Until those last notes faded away
Ending these love songs and stories
All that is left is two wedding rings

The Turning Point

Kuntala Bhattacharya

Jessica

Jessica was born in a small hill station at the foothills of the Himalayas. Her father was the owner of one of the prominent tea estates in the town. Her mother assisted in the daily operations of the tea estate.

She was four months old when her parents brought her to this place. Jessica was a quiet and loving child, adored by all the employees of the tea estate.

She used to play and dance around the tea gardens with her mother and her nanny. Her father occasionally came over from his daily schedule to watch his daughter. He would pick up small Jessica in his arms, tickle her cheeks and hug her. Jessica would giggle and her chuckling sound flowed through the air, enlightening everyone around.

"She is such a sweetheart, Maam. She will grow up to be a very bright and beautiful lady. God bless my dear child", Jessica's nanny Patricia would often tell her mother lovingly.

Patricia was an elderly lady in her 50's and was in charge of looking after Jessica since she was 5 months old. Both had a strong bonding between themselves which was an assurance for both Jessica's parents. They wanted someone like Patricia since they had to concentrate much on expanding the growth of their tea estate.

"Thank you, Patricia. Jessica is very fond of you. We are very happy, pleased, and thankful to you for your care and love for our daughter," smiled Jessica's mother, pressing Patricia's palms with gratitude.

"Do not worry, Maam. As long as I am there, Jessica will be safe. She is such a dear child," said Patricia with a soft voice.

Since her childhood, Jessica had a very strong capacity of capturing people's hearts with love. She mingled with everyone pleasingly. Her smile had immense purity which was captivating and enticing.

Being a woman with substantial experience in life, Patricia sometimes used to be worried about Jessica's attractive personality. She knew how the world can be cruel as well as polite. But she never spoke out her worry in front of Jessica's parents. She was aware that they had enough stress and tension with their business. Adding into their daughter's worry may unnerve them unnecessarily. Hence she avoided the conversation altogether instead kept herself completely engrossed in the well-being of Jessica.

The Fairyland

Patricia used to spend her entire day with Jessica, narrating to her all the famous fairy tales of eminent authors. Jessica listened to each of them attentively.

She imagined herself as one of the princesses or the fairies or the beautiful characters in the tales. Her mind drifted towards an imaginary fairyland with magnificent kingdoms and palaces. She dreamt of herself as a girl draped in dresses with glittering gems and artistic embroideries.

The stories of handsome princes arriving in white horses to rescue their beloved amazed her the most.

"Nanny, will a prince be coming for me too? Will he come galloping in a horse after traveling through countries, lands, rivers, oceans, and forests? Is there a demon or a dragon around our kingdom?" Jessica often asked Patricia inquisitively.

"Oh, my sweetheart. I think a smart good looking prince is waiting for you somewhere in the woods. He is waiting for the right moment to fight it out with the demons. Soon he will arrive victorious, riding in a marvelous horse with white flowing manes. And once he is here, he will be spellbound to see such a beautiful loving girl who stays in the palace of tea gardens," smiled Patricia, hugging Jessica. She lovingly caressed Jessica's cheeks and stroked her brownish lustrous hair.

Jessica felt overjoyed by being reassured by her nanny's words. She would tug herself into Patricia's lap, "Oh Nanny, I love you so much. It will be sad to leave you. But as you know I can't disappoint my prince. I have to go with him. But I will come often to visit you. You also have to come to my palace where I will be the queen."

Patricia would smile at her innocence. She sincerely prayed to God, "God protect my little child from all the problems and complexities in life. Let her live her dream the way she wants. Please guide her in her future."

Jessica remained engulfed in the thrilling and astonishing fairy tales. Every day she waited for her parents to sit with her when she could narrate them the stories and her dreams. Her parents listened to each of her story lovingly. They thanked Patricia with all their heart, "Patricia, Jessica had learned the stories so well. She seemed to be floating in the fairylands with the lovely characters. She has mingled herself into their spectacular lives."

"Mommy, Daddy, my prince will come soon. Promise me, you won't cry. Or else I will be very sad," Jessica often explained to her parents.

Her parents knew even if it's not a prince, someday Jessica might meet a handsome, smart, intelligent boy. She had to tie the knot and leave them. They knew it would be tough to part from their daughter. But they prayed to God for their little daughter to live life like a fairy tale with all the joy and happiness.

The Beginning Of A New Life

Jessica grew up to be a pretty young lady. She completed school and college and expressed her desire to be a fashion designer.

Her parents supported her desire. But the little hill station where they stayed did not have ample good opportunities for fashion design. Jessica had to shift to the metro city to start her career and earn recognition.

The thought of moving to the city was a concern for her parents and Patricia. Being brought up in a remote town, they knew it would be tough for her to adjust to the complexities of city life. They were unable to figure out the solution, on one side it was her career and on another side was her safety.

"Nanny, maybe if I move to the city my prince will arrive soon. I waited for so many years but maybe he is not able to trace where I am. I feel he will be able to find me soon if I stay in the city. I can pursue my career as well as my dreams," Jessica tried to reassure Patricia one night, looking aimlessly at the starry sky.

Patricia suddenly felt very sad for her little munchkin. She wiped her tears and hugged Jessica, "You may be right Jessica. But how can we leave you alone in the unknown city? There are enormous hardships and issues in a city. People of different characters and attitudes reside in metros. How will you adjust to them? We are so worried. Let us first find out a good place and some known people whom we can trust. We want to be reassured of your safety. I hope you understand Jessica".

"Yes Nanny, I understand," said Jessica sadly.

After enquiring through various acquaintances, Patricia could connect to one of her distant relatives staying in the city. The family, the Smiths, had migrated to the city long years back. They had a well-established family background and were one of the known noble families in the city.

Patricia connected Jessica's parents with the Smiths. Both families had a very respectful conversation. The Smiths provided them an address of a nearby apartment where Jessica can stay. The apartment was near to their house and if needed Jessica can always knock for any help.

Assured, Jessica's father arranged for her stay in one of the houses in the apartment. Along with Patricia and the help from the Smiths, Jessica's parents were able to settle her well. After staying with her for about a month, they departed back to the hills. In one month, Jessica got introduced to her new firm where she had been offered a job. Slowly she became conversant with city life.

Jessica thus started off her new journey of life with grace and dignity, the dream about her prince still embedded within her heart and mind.

The Breaking News

Jessica excelled in her work. She became one of the favorites of her boss, Ms. Daisy. Ms. Daisy was convinced with her dedication, sincerity, and intelligence. She asked Jessica to accompany her in most of her fashion shows.

It was Monday morning, Ms. Daisy summoned Jessica to her office cabin.

"Good Morning Maam, shall I come in?" asked Jessica, knocking and peeping at her boss's cabin.

"Oh very good morning, my dear lady. Please come in," greeted Ms. Daisy with a warm smile.

"Please be seated, Jessica. I have some sizzling good news for you," Ms. Daisy's voice chirped in excitement.

"What is it Maam? I am eager to hear it," Jessica asked, unable to control her excitement too.

"Finally and finally, I have decided you be the lead designer for this year's Daisy's Mega International Fashion Show. How is that Jessica?" answered Ms. Daisy with a super thrilling voice.

"Oh my God, what a pleasant surprise. Oh, Maam I am so thankful to you. This is indeed a great opportunity for me. I am so much privileged today. It's your extreme kindness to shower your trust and faith on me," Jessica jumped up with joy like a little girl.

"Aww Jessica come on. You deserve it. Now come here and give me a nice big hug. We need to have coffee together," said Ms. Daisy, lifting herself off her chair.

They hugged each other warmly and went for some coffee.

Jessica had a huge task at her disposal. The Mega Fashion Show was due within a month and there was a stupendous list of activities to be completed before that. Patricia decided to come and stay over with her during this hectic period. Jessica was very happy to hear about her arrival and started off her work with new zeal and excitement.

The Arrival Of The Prince

One month went away very fast. The day of the Mega International Fashion show arrived. Jessica looked a bit nervous, though she had completed all the arrangements perfectly.

Her parents too came over for the show. Jessica had specially invited the Smiths for the show. They had been a great help for her during this one month, assisting her with many acquaintances.

"Nanny, do I look good? I am so nervous today. I hope I can perform well. The team is creative and intelligent. But it is my first performance in such an internationally acclaimed fashion show," Jessica's voice trembled.

"Jessica, you are looking stunning my dear," her mother smiled at her as she entered her room.

"Yes Maam, you are right. Jessica, my child, you are looking like a fairy today. Who knows your prince may arrive today riding in a horse and pick you up in his arms?" giggled Patricia.

"Oh Nanny, you are such a sweetheart. Mommy, I am so glad that you and Daddy came over. I needed the strength and support today," said Jessica, lovingly looking up to the two most precious women of her life.

"Now Jessica, hurry up, you need to leave. We will reach before the show starts," said her mother.

Ms. Daisy had arranged for a car for Jessica and her family. Jessica reached the show premises and left the car to pick up her parents and Patricia.

The show started at the stipulated time. It was a spectacular show with prominent models and live music. Jessica performed remarkably well. She looked phenomenal with a lovely blue-colored gown sparkling with the beads and jewelry, especially self-designed by her for the occasion.

Jessica's parents and Patricia were seated at the front seat. Their eyes were full of pride as they watched Jessica arrive in intervals with the fashion models to be introduced as the lead designer. The Smiths were also seated beside them along with their son, who had arrived after his business tour from Australia.

As the lights focused on the audience, Jessica glanced towards the front seat to find her parents and Patricia. She smiled at them. Her eyes for a while deviated towards an unknown face. The man was handsome, smart, and dressed up in western formals. His gaze was fixed at Jessica which unnerved her a bit. But then she composed herself and bowed down before the audience gracefully to end the show finale.

"Who is he? And why was he staring at me? Is he the son of the Smiths? Let me not guess. Why should I bother, huh?" Jessica spoke to herself as she left the concert hall for her dressing room.

The Courtship

Jessica was granted a day off the next day to relax and spend time with her parents. Jessica's parents planned to invite the Smiths for dinner.

It was 6 PM when the Smiths came over to Jessica's apartment with their son.

"Hello, Mr. Smith. How are you doing today, Mrs. Smith? Thank you so much for coming in," greeted Jessica's father.

"It's our pleasure, Mr. Wilson," smiled Mr. Smith, exchanging greetings.

"Let me introduce our son, Harry. He had been on a business assignment for 2 years in Australia. The assignment is over and he had returned. We told him to come over with us," Mrs. Smith introduced her son to all.

"Very nice to meet you, Harry. Please come in," ushered Jessica's father.

Jessica was in her room attending a call on her mobile. She finished off and entered the living room. Her eyes immediately caught the attention of the same man seating in the front seat and constantly gazing at him. Now she understood who he was and felt a bit awkward too.

"Hello Jessica, how are you? You must be very tired after yesterday's show. Well, I must tell you. You were fabulous. We enjoyed it a lot. And Mrs. Wilson your daughter is a genius," said Mrs. Smith with a loving smile.

"Thank you, aunty, your blessings are important for me to progress further," answered Jessica respectfully.

"Oh, I forgot to introduce. This is my son Harry. And Harry this is Jessica. He too attended the show yesterday with us," Mrs. Smith introduced both.

Composing herself Jessica greeted Harry. She could feel the awkwardness in Harry's eyes too.

"You both can go over to the balcony and chit-chat. You will feel bored sitting here with us old fellows," said Jessica's father.

Jessica and Harry went and sat on the balcony. For 2 minutes none of them spoke.

Harry broke the silence, "Umm I am sorry for yesterday. I know it was a bit embarrassing to stare at you in that manner. But it was a wonderful experience and you were looking quite impressive. Sorry again."

"Oh no, that's fine," replied Jessica reassuringly.

They inquired about each other's profession. Jessica found herself very comfortable speaking with Harry. They spoke about their childhood and laughed at funny incidents.

Harry was mesmerized by Jessica's beauty, innocence, and intelligence. Jessica unknowingly shared many incidents of her childhood and professional life. She felt a close bond with Harry.

Before parting off for dinner, they exchanged each other's phone numbers and promised to ring up.

That was the starting of their relationship of love. They met almost every day and spent ample time with each other. Between their work and while at home they spoke for hours. A strong attraction and feeling encapsulated them and finally, they decided to be life partners.

"Nanny, finally my prince has arrived and is ready to take me to his palace of happiness," Jessica opened about her courtship with Harry to Patricia for the first time. She called up Patricia the day Harry asked her hand in marriage.

"Aww Jessica, is your prince our Harry?" Patricia's voice sounded glowing with excitement.

"Oh my God, how did you guess? It is from Harry, Nanny. I never imagined someone can love me so much. I am very happy, Nanny," answered Jessica with joy.

"Oh my dear child, I am happy too. So finally our princess will be married to the great prince and escorted to his kingdom where soon she would be the queen of her palace," laughed Patricia as tears rolled down her cheeks.

That day Jessica could not sleep. She looked up at the sky and spoke to her imaginary fairy godmother.

"Do you listen to me fairy godmother? My prince has come looking for me. He is handsome and smart. He doesn't have a horse though. I can adjust to that. Haha. He loves me so much. I love him too. I am the queen of the Fairyland," Jessica danced and danced and danced.

The Marriage

Jessica and Harry did not face any difficulty in convincing their parents about their marriage. Both families were extremely pleased with each other. They had immense faith in Jessica and Harry.

A date was finally fixed for their marriage. The marriage was to be held in Jessica's hometown. Both the families wanted it to be a grand celebration. They selected an open-air resort at the backdrop of the green majestic mountains as the marriage venue.

Jessica's parents transformed the entire place into a magical kingdom. They knew of their daughter's dreams. They connected with the finest of the interior decorator firms for the mystic creations.

Harry's mother was initially hesitant about the thought, "A kingdom? For a marriage party? Isn't it a bit strange? I mean we have our traditional methods to celebrate. Those are a kid's fairy tale stories".

But Harry convinced her, "But Mom, think about the uniqueness. It will be a different experience. Let's accept the positive part of it".

Jessica and Harry's marriage was packed with all the grandeur of luxury and happiness. The hills seemed to be glorified with the beauty of Jessica and her handsome prince Harry. Family and friends blessed the newlywed couple.

Amidst tears, hugs, and kisses and spending the next 4 days with her parents and Patricia, Jessica bid goodbye to them. She held Harry's hand while being escorted into the car.

Jessica stepped into the world of marriage. Parting with her parents and especially Patricia was difficult. But her dreams of childhood had, at last, come true. She was embarking on her journey as a queen with her beloved prince. Harry hugged her closely and kissed her forehead. Jessica tugged herself in his warmth. There was peace, there was tranquility and there was serenity.

Jessica closed her eyes and engulfed herself into the calmness; slowly captivating her mind and soul.

The Confrontation

Jessica entered the mansion of the Smiths. She was astounded by its architectural magnificence and artistic sculptures.

She started to feel like a princess to be transformed into a queen.

"Do you like my palace, Jessica?" whispered Harry into her ears.

"Of course I do, Harry. It is such a marvelous place. I am honored," Jessica whispered back.

Jessica could not wait to ring up Patricia and her parents, explaining to them every detail of the mansion. She was so excited to talk about her dream fairyland.

"Nanny, a new fairy tale needs to be written; *Jessica in her Fairyland*. What do you say?" giggled Jessica as she spoke with Patricia over the phone.

Patricia laughed, "Oh yes we have to, my dear child. I am so happy for you. My baby has finally become a queen".

Days passed with visits from friends and relatives. There were occasional cocktail parties to entertain the guests and introduce them to the newlywed couple. Not a single guest left the place without praising the charming nature of Jessica.

Slowly and steadily, both Jessica and Harry had to settle down with their daily routine life. Before marriage, Jessica used to pack her lunch before leaving for work. As a matter of habit, she went to the kitchen to pack her lunch.

"Jessica dear, what are you doing in the kitchen? Aren't you supposed to be dressing up for your work?" Mrs. Smith spotted Jessica entering the kitchen and enquired.

"Oh yes, Mom. I am just packing my lunch," answered Jessica politely.

"Jessica, this is not your parent's place or your apartment where you used to stay. This is a place equivalent to a palace. Only servants enter the kitchen of a palace. You have to converse with the family etiquettes. I don't want people to laugh at you," there was a sudden sternness in Mrs. Smith's voice.

Jessica was surprised. She had never encountered such strictness in Mrs. Smith's voice. But she obeyed, "I am sorry, Mom. I understand. I will ensure it is not repeated."

"That's better. Sarah, pack the lunch box of Jessica", Mrs. Smith ordered the maid.

Jessica felt a bit sad but she adjusted to the change. She thought maybe she was thinking too much. These are small things that could be easily be forgotten.

The past days had gone by with the visitors and the family never got the opportunity to dine together.

The same day in the evening, after both Jessica and Harry had returned from their respective workplace, the family met at the dinner table.

Though Jessica knew all the courtesies of dining, at home she was quite casual with her parents. She used to chat with her parents and sit cozily with her dinner plate.

The moment she stepped into the dining area, it felt odd. The table and the chairs were arranged in a very formal manner as if anticipating arrival of guests. The plates and the cutlery were aligned the way usually done in parties.

She silently observed the process. Harry's father sat at the head of the table facing others. Harry's mother, Harry, and Jessica then sat the chairs alongside. She watched them following all the patterns of decency and felt uncomfortable.

"Is it very necessary for us to follow all the formalities when it's only us and no outsiders? Why can't we chat and sit together and dine?" Jessica suddenly spoke out.

Mr. and Mrs. Smith gave a stern look at her face. Harry pressed her hand as a signal to stop speaking.

"Jessica, there are some rules which you need to follow. Life here is different than what you have led before. Harry, did you not explain everything? I thought you had already done that," Mr. Smith sounded very strict.

"I am sorry Dad. Everything will be fine. I will explain to Jessica," reassured Harry.

A sudden silence hovered at the dining table. Everyone finished dinner and departed to sleep.

The Reality

The next few months were a grueling experience for Jessica. The rules and boundaries made her tired. It seemed someone has imprisoned her, tied up with heavy chains inside some remote abandoned house.

Her dream mansion turned out to be a witch's fort. The magnificence of the mansion soon appeared gruesome and dull. Her freedom and independence were being snatched away from her. She felt suffocated inside the mansion. Her prince of happiness, Harry, was slowly converting into a stranger.

Harry's parents were annoyed with Jessica's denials and reasons. They expressed dissatisfaction with her behavior and activities.

Jessica had expected Harry to be upfront and smart. But he turned out to be different. He never supported Jessica in her arguments of leading a simple and cozy life at home. The outside life, according to Jessica, could be formal. Inside the house, all family members must be cordially bonded with each other. Harry and his parents never understood Jessica nor even tried to.

The distance between Jessica and Harry increased more and more each day.

"Nanny, I was such a fool to believe that my life will be similar to one of the fairy tales. Fairy tales are meant to be in dreams only. In reality, life is far tougher. I understood now in a very harsh manner," sighed Jessica as she called up Patricia.

"Oh No, Jessica. Please don't talk like that. It's my fault that I narrated all those fairy tales. I should not have done so. Oh My God. My child, please be steady and calm," Patricia seemed very worried.

"No Nanny, it is not your fault. Many children listen to fairy tales, don't they? But I did a mistake in connecting those stories to my life. Don't be worried. The only problem is I will not survive if I allow the suffocation to continue. I need to decide my life now or never," Jessica's voice sounded firm.

Patricia and Jessica's parents had never seen Jessica so stern and firm. They were concerned but somehow they did not interfere. They waited patiently for her decision.

The Final Decision

It was 6 PM on a Sunday. Jessica had requested her parents and Patricia to come over to the Smiths. She had earlier requested permission from the Smiths for the invitation. They had agreed reluctantly.

Jessica, Harry, Patricia, and both their parents were seated in the huge living room area.

"Sorry for summoning all of you suddenly. You must be wondering why. Well yes, there is a reason for my request," Jessica started to speak.

"I am a different human being, not like a typical girl who can adjust to all the norms of family life or the grandeur of a noble family. I have a free-flowing mind and a heart full of innocent and simple desires. I do respect all of your beliefs, traditions, and customs. But I want to live my life the way I want. If I stay in this way I am being forced to be with, I may not survive long. I don't want to be the fate of a forced destiny. Hence I have decided to end this marriage gracefully. Harry is a talented and smart man. He could soon find himself a girl who can fit into the traditions. I am not that person who you all are looking for. I am sorry for everything. Please do not try to stop me as this is my final decision. I have lots to do and work on in the future. Thanks for all your support till today", Jessica sighed a heavy breath.

There was absolute silence in the whole room. With a few formalities over dinner, the day ended.

Jessica excused herself from dinner and went to her room. She went to the balcony, "Oh fairy godmother, I have told them everything. I want to live. I want to fly. I want to dance. I want to breathe fresh air. Give me power. Give me the strength". Jessica burst into tears.

A twinkling reflection in the sky made her wipe off her tears and gaze at the sky. Her fairy godmother has arrived.

Jessica knew she has received the blessings of her fairy godmother.

After the separation, Jessica moved to a new apartment. She worked hard and set up her firm on Fashion designing. Ms. Daisy, her ex-boss, assisted her a lot in setting up her new venture. Jessica's fame spread worldwide. She earned recognition among the prestigious international fashion designers.

Awards and accolades poured on her as Jessica achieved the heights of glory.

"Nanny, I have changed my dream a bit. Do you see my fairyland? There it is," Jessica pointed at the beautiful lovely house she had built with her belongings.

Friendship is love

James Kinsella

Prologue

Friendship is love

A field of dreams

Uniting two souls

Into one stream

As butterflies circle the fields of dreams

You will find you and me cuddled in love

Holding tight to those golden themes

Watching those fields grow our love

Were the grass growing high and no end
There we sit and look at the sky
Thinking how great our love is as friends
Knowing underneath, it's as warm as a blue sky

As the clouds roll by, as the sunset fading
Things will never change between our cravings
When the day fades and the night begins
Those times that are ours will begin

Somewhere between the circles of day and night
With a song in our hearts and a kiss on our lips
We will unite our two circles in highlights
And tomorrow, our bond will steer our ship

The Monk Of Tholung Gompa

Dipannita Bhattacherya

The Invitation and the Excitement

"Am I reading it correctly?" I had said to myself.

I remember I had read the email more than ten times. Each time I was going through it, I wanted to reconfirm if I was reading it correctly.

I was invited to the 'Kamsil Ceremony' at Sikkim's mystical monastery, the eighteenth-century old, Tholung Gompa. The festival takes place once every three years. The Tholung Gompa is located at 8000 feet above sea level in the remotest of Lepcha paradise, upper

Dzongu. It lies in the outskirts of the Khangchendzonga National Park, a UNESCO World Heritage Site. It is a global biodiversity hot spot.

Khangchendzonga National Park, nestled in core Eastern Himalayas, is a dense ancient forest, including World's third-highest peak, the sacred Khangchendzonga. Myths and mystery rule this part of the world. This is what intrigues me beside the breathtakingly scenic views.

At the Kamsil Ceremony the unveiling of some ancient sacred relics to the public, which otherwise are preserved in boxes, are done by the Ecclesiastical Affairs Department of the Government of Sikkim. It is said that some of the relics belonged to Guru Rinpoche or Padmasambhava, the eighth-century Buddhist master. He carried Buddhism from India to Tibet and is considered 'The Second Buddha'.

Even though Tholung Gompa is so significant and one of the most sacred Buddhist monasteries in India, it is not so popular among tourists for its obscure location. Why obscure? Well, I am coming to that. This was indeed a prestigious invitation. I was excited but for me, there was something much more than just the invitation.

I have had the opportunity of staying in various gompas or Buddhist monasteries. I consider myself blessed to have come in the vicinity of many revered monks or lamas. Their simplicity and methods of being one with nature always attract me. However, this time it was a little different and so was I super excited.

My excitement knew no bounds, not only for having a chance of being witness to such a sacred and unique ceremony but also because I would finally get to meet the hundred years old reverend Lama Yonten Dorje.

I had tried meeting him while working on 'Folklore and Religion' but did not succeed. In the summers he often lives alone in the caves and ruins of an ancient gompa a few kilometers above Tholung. It is said that the ruins have prophetic mention and that Rinpoche or Guru Padmasamvabha's footprints still exist and are preserved.

Lama Yonten Dorje is believed to possess enormous powers through years of mastering the art of tantra. Rumors have it that he flies above the snow-clad Himalayan peaks to control the evil spirits of the mountains. His guardian spirit is the 'Migoi', the yeti, the mysterious abominable snowman. He was a six-year-old boy found in the caves.

The then prevailing head of Tholung Gompa had a dream of this boy being attended to by the yeti. His dream also confirmed that this boy was special. On his instructions, people found him out and brought him to Tholung. Few years after his training, he became the head of Tholung Gompa by the age of sixteen. Buddhist monks believe in dreams, incarnations, and rebirth and practice many other Tantric forms of worship which are different from ordinary ways of our regular life.

The Journey

All the guests first had to arrive at Gangtok, the capital city of Sikkim. We were a team of seven guests from all across India. There were other guests and foreign delegates who had already left for Thonlung the day before we started. We traveled for six hours, from Gangtok to Lingzey, a Himalayan hamlet, where we stayed the night at the Village Head's house. This is the last point accessible by a motorable road.

From Lingzey it is a trek of 6 hours to reach Tholung. However, for the festival, the monastery had arranged palanquins and porters for the senior guests. Our team preferred to trek.

The next morning we began our trek at four, through paddy fields at first, entering into forests. We crossed ice-cold narrow streams and bamboo bridges over the gushing Rimpi River. Some of the narrow bamboo bridges were ten to twelve inches wide. The dry river bed had slippery boulders.

The trek was risky. The trek through the rocky landslide zone for about two hours was the most dangerous part of the journey. This part of the Himalayas is extremely steep. Then in the last league of the trek, we hiked through the dense coniferous forest again. It was dark, mossy, and damp. The pines, the rhododendrons, their smell, the birds' calls, and the gurgling sound of flowing streams, together with the mist weaved magic.

We seemed to be walking in some other world. There were colorful prayer flags, fluttering even in the deepest parts of the forest.

"Who comes and ties them here?" I thought.

At clearings, we stood mesmerized at the majestic peak of Kangchendzonga and other snow-capped mountains. I could stand and stare at the mountain peaks in awe for several hours.

On the way through the forest, a few locals started joining us. They were heading towards the monastery too. They carried pine dhoop, burning incense made from very high-altitude pine twigs, which filled the air with an intoxicating smell.

Most of the adults had prayer beads in their hands or handheld mani *wheels* or prayer wheels which they kept churning together with chanting mantras. They didn't look tired and their eyes glittered with enthusiasm. These simple and rustic villagers have limited opportunities for a celebration unlike what we city people have.

Suddenly we heard the sound of the gongs, horns, and drums. We realized that we had almost reached the monastery.

The Kamsil Ceremony And The Festivities

Surprisingly we didn't look exhausted even after a six hours' trek because the spirit of the place was of fun and festivities. Some of the locals had dressed up colorfully in their traditional silk woven robes.

The monastery was freshly painted. The frescos and murals of Tibetan gods on the walls looked alive. Huge thangkas hang and there were colorful prayer flags, fluttering all around. Even a few ornamented yaks grazed near the monastery.

There were few visitors in comparison to that of festivals at popular gompas.

"Less crowd is good; helps in preserving nature's bliss", I thought.

I was at the Hemis Festival once, at Hemis Monastery, Ladakh. I had also visited the 'Black-necked Crane Festival' at Gangtey Gompa in Phobjhikha, Bhutan. I have been to quite a few Buddhist festivals in the popular monasteries. Their crowd and the pomp and show are past compare.

Here, at Tholung, the scale of celebration was minimal. There hardly was a crowd. Revered religious guests and top officials from Ministry were present. We were welcomed with a traditional scarf and served salty butter tea and Lepcha lunch.

I was amazed to see the faith in the eyes of these people when some of the ancient relics were being held up publicly. I kept on thinking of their antique values.

There were rhythmic chanting, music, and mask dances by the monks. This dance called 'Chham', is a performance reflecting gods driving away the demons. The place was full of joy and energy. Children played and danced and the adults laughed their hearts out. We kept clicking photos to our hearts' contents.

The Museum And Library Of Tholung Monastery

When the locals started dispersing, Lama Dechen Yeshe, the Administrative Head, started meeting the guests. Some had already left.

At this hour the guests, including me, who were at the Tholung Gompa were invited to stay the night over.

I had met Lama Dechen on a few occasions before. I bowed to him, touched his feet, and requested him earnestly, *"Could I once grace the blessing of Lama Yonten Dorje, please. I wanted to meet him for years but was never successful."*

He replied, "I can not promise but I will try. Right now he has retired to his chamber. He is too old for meeting visitors."

Then he instructed a young Lama to show us around the monastery including the museum and library and left promising that he would meet us over dinner.

The library and museum is the most intriguing part of the monastery. My heart pounded to see such age-old manuscripts. There are seals from the era of Emperor Asoka. It was astonishing to see that such a prized collection was not under the surveillance of cameras.

Electricity is yet to arrive here. On questions about the security of the museum and library to the young lama, he pointed at two huge Tibetan mastiffs wagging their tails. Even a dog lover like me was shaken by their size and the burning look in their eyes.

The young lama confidently said, *"These gentle giants guard the space. Any mishandling and you don't know what you run into. They can tear one to pieces with their sharp fangs."*

"Of course, I understand", I said.

I spent some time there just admiring these hidden treasures. Ancient manuscripts, seals, thangkas made with gold, flutes made of yak bones, musical instruments, and other carvings from yak horns, silver conches, jade cups, and numerous other priceless items filled the place.

The young lama showed me a manuscript with details of the medicinal use of almost all Himalayan plants. He also showed me tantric manuscripts which explained how to use inner shakti or power with that of nature to act in manners which we, the common people would call magical. Well, I clearly understood that just a few hours at this library is not enough.

Dinner Time

We were called for dinner at eight in the evening. Walking through the alleys of the gompa with a lit lantern was eerie. We often mistook our long shadows as someone following us.

The huge frescos in the walls did not seem welcoming. The wind blowing through the pines made a heart-wrenching sound. Once we entered the dining hall and kitchen, we felt comfortable. The room was warm from the fire of the large Chulha, the fire oven made of mud where the fire was lit using wood and coal.

We sat on the floor and were served a simple dinner; rice, squash curry, and a soup prepared with fresh cabbage and carrots. They served us 'Churpi ka achar' which is a pickle made with yak cheese. The simple dinner tasted heavenly because all the ingredients were fresh and organic.

Lama Dechen Yeshe did not eat with us but visited us. He asked us about our day at Tholung and after talking a bit about the monastery announced, *"Tomorrow morning the reverend Lama Yonten Dorje will bless all of you."*

"Yes, Finally!" I exclaimed with child-like joy. Lama Dechen questioned with a smile, *"Why do you want to meet him so badly?"* I replied breathlessly, *"Because he had met the yeti and from my childhood, I am obsessed with yeti."* Everyone shared a good laugh.

However, Lama Dechen did not. Instead, he seriously said, *"Yeti is no myth as considered by the western world. Yeti demands respect for it appears and disappears of its own will. It assumes various forms. Not everyone gets to see it. Who sees a yeti is predestined. Only a pure soul is blessed by it. Lama Yonten says that the Yeti was once the keeper of this monastery. It exists even today but doesn't succumb to civilized skeptics. He will be happy to know that there is a believer among us."* Most of the others did not seem much interested in the Yeti story.

The Dawn

Anxiousness kept me awake through the night. I was out on the porch before the break of dawn. Sunrise and the Khangchendzonga have a divine bonding. The picture of the changing colors of the glistening snow-clad peak, from purple to pink, red, and then golden during the sunrise remains etched in memory forever.

I stood admiring the first rays of the sun on the snow-white peaks when suddenly I felt there was someone behind. I turned to find the revered Lama Yonten. My heart stopped for a moment and then it started beating aloud. For once I thought I could hear my heartbeat.

I ran towards him. The old man stood still; smiling at me; looking into my eyes. I was sure he was looking beyond my eyes. He could see through my heart, mind, and soul. As I approached closer he said with a smile, *"The more we doubt the more we lose our connection with nature. We are losing touch."*

I touched his feet. He placed his hand on my head and then something unusual happened. His palm felt so heavy on my head that I could not move. I could not raise my head to see what suddenly happened. My eyes were almost closing. I was bent down in the posture required to touch someone's feet. I am sure I saw a pair of large brownish furry human-like legs with huge feet.

"Lama where are you? Who is this?" I tried to scream as I could feel that the Lama was gone and some huge furry figure stood in front of me.

However, the weight and force of the palm on my head were so irresistibly strong that I could neither move nor speak any more.

"Is this a bear or is this the Yeti? How did it come here? I have to look for the Lama", I thought. There was an intoxicating smell similar to that of the pine and rhododendron forests here and I slowly lost my senses. Most likely I fell unconscious.

I opened my eyes and found a few inquisitive faces looking down upon me. Lama Dechen was also there. I jumped up but couldn't tell people of my unbelievable experience. Everyone wanted to know what had happened.

I said, "*I woke up before dawn and slipped in the dark and lost consciousness. There's nothing to worry about. I feel fine now*"

Lama Dechen instructed, *"If you feel alright then come with me to Lama Yonten. I want to begin with you. He will bless the guests one by one. You will get to meet him finally."* Without being able to hide my enthusiasm, I remarked, *"We have already met this morning."* To this, Lama Dechen confirmed, *"You must have been dreaming for he was in his private prayer chamber since four am in the morning."* I kept quiet.

We reached the main hall of the gompa where Lama Yonten was seated on the brocaded Grand Abbot's seat. He was chanting on prayer beads in his left hand and was churning the mani wheel in the right. The room was smoky with burning dhoops. I could smell that hypnotic smell of the mountains and forests again. I was getting into some kind of trance when it was broken by Lama Dechen's voice.

Lama Dechen bowed before Lama Yonten and pointing towards me told, *"This is the Yeti lover I told you about."*

Lama Yonten smiled with the same intent look. I am sure he knew what I was thinking. He knew about my confusion from the morning. The innumerable wrinkles on his face stretched a little more.

He said smiling mischievously, *"O I have already blessed her in the morning while I was praying at my secret praying chamber"*. I stood speechless and Lama Dachen smiled showing me forward.

With slow and shivering steps I touched Lama Yonten's feet and he placed his palm on my head to bless me. The moment I looked at him with doubtful eyes, the old revered Lama said, *"Do not have doubts. I am old but my memory is still strong. I have already blessed you in the morning"*.

Then he giggled like a kid and winked at me.

The Sight of You

James Kinsella

Keen moonlight flows on your hair
As bright as dazzling angels' flares
Golden as your locks of hair
Laying upon your shoulders bare

It was this moonlight that brought me there
To see an angel walking in a moonlit night
Knowing at once my heart became bare
That I have fallen in love catching an angel's sight

Melody Of A Piano And Scent Of Jasmine

Dipannita Bhattachherya

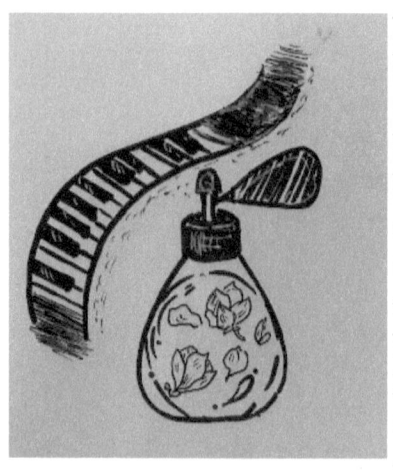

Today morning as I stood at the balcony, sipping my cuppa, I found that furniture from the house exactly beside the one I lived in, being brought out on the road. There stood a truck on which these were being transferred. It seemed my next-door neighbour was shifting. It has just been two months that I came to this house in Salt Lake, after my transfer from Siliguri; and to my dismay, just after four days, the lockdown for the pandemic was announced. I haven't been able to meet a single neighbour. However, I know that I have an extremely skilled pianist as my next door neighbour. I have heard someone in that house playing piano almost all day. The packers and movers brought out the grand piano too.

Whenever I drowned into the puddle of soft notes on the piano from the next door, I have always imagined an elegant lady as the pianist. The pianist must be a lady because my nose often caught upon a feminine fragrance of a floral perfume, most probably jasmine, whenever I stood by the window trying to intently listen to the melodic piano. The musician is gifted. Due to stringent rules during the lock down I could never gather the courage to ring their doorbell and ask, "Hello, I am your new next-door neighbour. Who from your house, plays such soulful music?"

Today I found the perfect opportunity and ran down to the road to find out who she was.

A middle-aged lady stood supervising the packing and shifting of the furniture. I approached her with a smile, "Hi, I live next door. I moved in just four days before the lockdown started. So we have never met before." She smiled and nodded.

I added, "Are you shifting? I want to thank whoever played the piano throughout the lockdown. It was therapeutic. I see the piano outside. I will definitely miss such melody."

The lady frowned and blasted, "Is this some kind of joke? Don't you know that the house was empty for last three months? We had sold the house two months back, just after my mom's death. The packers and movers could not be arranged because of the lockdown. So finally, we are getting it done today."

Confused and humiliated I said, "Sorry! I really didn't know a thing. I had no clue that there was no one in the house."

As I turned to leave, the lady stopped me. "Sorry for being rude. This is my grand mom's piano handed down to my mom who was a gifted pianist."

I gathered myself and explained her how every day I heard the piano and also about the scent of the perfume I could smell from the window from where the piano really sounded loud and clear. I confessed that I could feel the piano being placed just on the other side of the window.

"She enjoyed playing the piano. I am sure she must have missed playing it in her last days which she spent with me in my house in Delhi. Her last wish must have been…anyway", the lady sighed. "I know you are not lying", she continued with tears in her eyes and a smile at the corner of her lips.

"I had gifted her favourite jasmine perfume the day before she expired. The pack is still sealed and lying in Delhi."

I always feel that we have exploited the earth enough to make it angry. The earth dreams of being free from our cruel selfish clutches and hence screams out these words…

Words From A Girl Called Eartha (Earth)

Dipannita Bhattacherya

I am a ghost inside,
Hiding my darkness within,
From people who can see only where the light shines.

Did I tell you that I love the rumble of dry leaves and scorpions?
And that my favourite colour is grey?
Did I tell you that I love the rugged and the ruined?
You have only seen those sparkling black rimmed dreamy eyes,
Behind those dreams, I hide them - large and round eyes full of tears.
I hide the tears with the spark and the smudged kohl.

The beautiful body you touch is not my nakedness you have felt.

It is far deeper, full of scratches and etches from the journey of life.

I am a dead inside,

Hiding the chained soul deep beneath,

From the people who call one alive only when they see their corpse move around.

Did I tell you that I am waiting for freedom,

Though you think I am free?

Did I tell you my body will burn to grey ashes for this life can offer no other colour?

However, my soul can, if unchained-

Into colours green and blue.

I wait for that day when my true dream will come true.

The Baptism

Johanny Ortega

Junior's baptism was on October 18, 2018. I came late to mass and unfortunately missed a six-month-old's involuntary participation in a ritual that was more pagan than Christian. I mean, using water as a purification tool to be born anew? Witchy much? No?

I mean, poor baby. He had no idea what he was getting into and most likely cried as some random stranger in a robe (who may or may not be a pedophile) poured cold water over his head. But to us Ramos family, it was a tale as old as time. Every year someone got married, then pregnant and pop. Then, just like that, poorly written text messages, non-stop phone calls, and a few brazen emails will let me know my presence is required at some relative's baptism. If I even hesitated one bit, my mother would make sure to let me know how the family I'm rejecting is the same one that came together so I could go to school. Super subtle, if you ask me. So as long as folks continue to pop, I travel. I should make that into a t-shirt.

I'm glad I stopped at the bathroom and missed the Uber who left me a nasty text. I'm glad I had to switch to Lyft and wait another twenty minutes. I missed little. Just another baptism.

I remember it was sticky hot that day. I heard later, the church, in all its wisdom, turned off the air conditioning. They figured it's fall; why not. But even if they would have turned it on, it wouldn't have mattered. Too many folks, not enough ventilation, it was a recipe for disaster, really.

Yeah, I was glad to be late. I missed the whispers that travel across the pews and somehow flutter in the air like innocent butterflies whose wings move in the same frantic rhythm as the folded hand fans. But those whispers weren't innocent, and neither are the butterflies. Unfortunately, I didn't miss the get-together.

I don't know why they call it that when it's almost like a second Navidad with the same amount of food, the same amount of people, and the same amount of gossip. I didn't even get to sit down on a foldable gray metal chair with the cushion slashed and gutted before a second aunt or third cousin called me over. "¿Muchachita pero tu eres la hija de Carmen, verdad?"

If we were closely related, she wouldn't have to ask me if my mother is Carmen. She would know. "Si," I said.

I remember I let out a small laugh like I always do when I'm around them.

"That's right, your mother didn't teach you Spanish," she commented after hearing my thick accent in the single syllable word.

I remember my cheeks growing warm and an uncomfortable drop of sweat gingerly rolling down my spine.

"It's okay." The lady whose position in my family tree I did not know looked over her shoulder and waved. "Mira, Yolanda, come see Carmen's daughter."

Of course, Yolanda doesn't come on her own. She drags three other ladies around the same age. You know the kind of age that makes your FUPA expand to your waist, makes you draw exaggerated lines around your lips to fill them in with scandalous red lipstick, tattoo thin brown lines into eyebrows and apply way too much eyeliner.

As they drew near, the pack of Dominican hyenas held on to the same half-curious, half judgmental stares. It is the same one most far away relatives have when they meet me, someone, who shares some of their genes but it's completely different. If the women were old-school calculators, I would have heard the paper churning fastidiously.

I remember the sweat cascading down my back now and finally settling on my crotch. I glanced over at my mother. She's not my biggest fan. She predicted I wouldn't get a job with a journalism degree. But she would at least come to my rescue. She knows terrible publicity for me was directly linked to her mothering skills. Unfortunately, she has immersed herself in whatever conversation junior's mom decided was important enough to hold her hostage.

As the Dominican hyenas surrounded me in a lethal circle. The murmurs grew in Spanish, English, and Spanglish. Those outside the kill circle shifted discreet eyes and fingers my way. At that moment, I was literally Simba. Do I fight or fly? The surrounding air grew thin, and I pulled my collar away from my neck. I laughed.

"Mire," said one woman in a bright red dress with a yellow flower-print before she pinched the fat that folded over the waist of my jeans. "A little fat? Ahi que cuidarse."

The audacity of someone with more rolls than the doughboy to tell me I have to watch what I eat. I fumed inside. But I laughed, of course.

Another hyena slapped the hand of the red dress woman. "You never know some men like that," she told her. The woman had two thin lines tattooed over her eyes, which I was sure served as her eyebrows. She drew near as in, conspiring in secret. "You have a boyfriend?"

After asking, she made a show of looking around, getting on her tiptoes, and looking over the heads of the hyena circle.

My jaw was clamped shut, so it took me a while to open my mouth. I didn't get to utter a word because the red lip hyena saw my hesitation as weakness and pounced.

"Why you ask her that?" she said. I loosened my jaw a little and looked at her. Some of the red lip transferred on her two front teeth. "It's 2018, Juanita. It may be a girlfriend. You never know."

At the hint of queerness, murmurs seized being whispered within the hyena circle. Suddenly, I was stuck in a pack of crying hyenas, as if they were about to make a meal out of me. My eyes darted around their lethal circle, tracing the curves of everybody within, looking for a gap, an opening, something. My nervous laugh grew tired, and before my throat ran dried, I found it; a hole within bodies, big enough for me and the rolls over my jeans to fit through.

"Nice to meet you, all," I said, so nothing can go back to my mother about me being rude to elders.

But the hyena elders were too busy talking to themselves on every which way my life may go and didn't see me squeeze through them. They didn't even hear me say anything.

I would be lying if I said I was going to sit in the sala where the men watched football. The OGs sat a few feet away by the kitchen to be close to food and still within the grace of the air conditioning god. Yeah, that would be a lie. The truth would be if I told you I was going to make a beeline towards the bathroom on my way out the door.

But the most astute one of all the hyenas caught me before I passed the threshold into the home. My mother hooked her arm to my elbow and pressed her lips to my ear. "Have you taken care of your situation?" she whispered.

I raised my chin and met my mother's eyes. Abortion was still a cursed word in my family, especially around El Padre enjoying a free meal on us. I've told her before about using too much eyeliner. Still, she never listened, and now in this heat, she was looking more like an angry raccoon than a hyena. The good thing was that words were not needed between her and me. She raised me by herself, and at one point, I raised myself. Within that span of raising, we developed a secret language.

Disappointed in a way only I could tell, my mother went back to talking too-fast-Spanish.

The blast of cold air welcomed me into the inner sanctum of the house—the kitchen. I passed the OG's with their veiny hands holding on to half-eaten plates they probably forget were on their laps. Every once in a while, someone would check on them. Do you want soda? More rice? Pollo? 'No, no, I'm fine', they would reply stubbornly and wait until the person would stop coming to check on them to complain no one did.

I passed the sala with the men sitting in two circles. The oldest of them sat on the couch, perfectly spaced because God forbid one man's thighs rubbed against the other. The youngish of them sat on the gray metal chairs they brought from outside.

Then I passed a man so miserable, he sat by no one at the corner of sala and hallway with his neck bent down over his phone watching some old school Bruce Willis movie. He was my people.

"Baño?" I asked him careful to pronounce the word with the tiniest bit of gringo accent.

He exhaled, paused the movie, and pointed with his chin down the hall.

When he moved, the man smelled like fried plantains. This was my favorite dish, and I was wondering how they'd run out so soon, but after getting a whiff, I wondered no more. I nodded, but the sudden movement made my stomach tumble. Soon vile threatened to rise from my throat and spill all over the black and white ceramic floor. I ambled forward, afraid any fast movement would expel the bagel I ate this morning. In what seemed like forever down the hallway, I reached a boy shuffling back and forth from foot to foot, holding on to his crutch.

The acid burned the back of my throat. I tap the boy's shoulder. "Please," I pleaded.

Right then, the door to the bathroom we were both waiting for opened. The boy zoomed in, almost knocking one of the OGs coming out. She leaned on her cane. I grabbed her elbow to steady her. Once the boy slammed the door behind him, the OG smiled at me. She had no teeth, and I wondered if she'd left them in the bathroom. Her cloudy eyes trailed my figure, and then she cupped my cheek. The vile stopped. I cover her hand with mine.

The OG's smile widened before she slipped her hand from my cheek. I felt the veins, loose skin, and raised liver spots slide through my palm. Shortly, warmth covered my womb, and I look down to find the veiny hand there. Our gazes locked. Her eyes were cloudy with too many years lived. Every line etched on her face seemed to be an experience she survived. The OG patted my womb gently. Her voice trembled the way old people's voices tremble. "Que bueno, another baptism."

Tick Tock

Elizabeth Anne Bryant

Tick Tock, Tick Tock
Goes the clock on the wall
Tick Tock, Tick Tock
Summer's gone it's fall
Time doesn't stop for anything, or for anyone
You hear the clock go Tick Tock, and then the day is done

Tick Tock, Tick Tock
Time is a fickle thing
Tick Tock, Tick Tock
Winter's gone it's Spring

You can't stop for anything, or for anyone
Because the clocks go Tick Tock, and then the day is done

Tick Tock, Tick Tock
Life goes fast enough
You don't have to rush it
You don't have to push it
Stop, Stop, Stop
You always have time to go forward
But you can never go backward
Because the clock always goes
Tick Tock, Tick Tock

Kiki's Cuckoo Clock

Elizabeth Anne Bryant

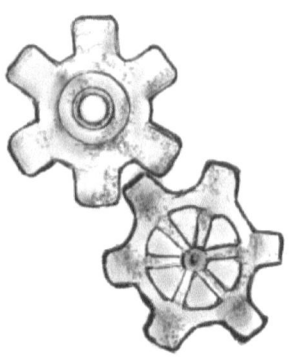

The room was drab and gray, the color it once had buried in rusting bits of metal and half-finished dreams, never to be realized. Among the workbenches that had become looming mountains of clutter, a small figure sat. Her greasy black hair matching her oil covered fingers and her stained overalls. Across the room, a door creaked open, revealing another woman in a fashionable pant suit and a slightly taller figure, though this was due mostly to her 6-inch pink heels. Her arms were laden with plastic grocery bags and her makeup-heavy face beamed a radiant smile.

"Hey sister! I brought goodies!" Without looking up from her work the hunched figure responded,

"Sister-in-law technically." The pink heeled woman's broad smile became strained, but she tried to bring the mood back up.

"It's just an expression Esmeralda, all of my gal-pals are sisters to me."

"Ahh," Esmeralda fiddled a bit with the pieces of metal in her hand, testing how well the joints would move to her will.

She did not look up.

The woman's face fell as she raised up the bags dangling off her arms.

"Where do you want these, Hun?" Esmerelda just shrugged. The bags crinkled harshly as the woman dropped her arms and rolled her eyes. "Well, you're gonna have to clear away something because there's not even enough room for a flea to sit without sitting on something." Her heels clopped and squeaked as she tried to shove a mix of rusting metal and yellowing papers out of the way with her unwieldy footwear, "There isn't even any floor space! The flea probably got trapped under a moldy newspaper and just got crushed by me."

Esmerelda tightened a loose bolt slightly and tried moving her makeshift hinge back and forth again. The woman was used to Esmerelda ignoring her and she continued speaking anyway.

"Did you make a machine that multiplies junk when I'm not looking?" She said sarcastically. She stumbled over to one of the workbenches with a mountain of scrap metal spilling over the edges and onto the concrete floor. "I'm dropping these bags on this pile of pipes and metal plate thingies. Is that okay?"

"Sure," Esmerelda was still trying to get the perfect amount of tightness on the bolt.

"Are you really sure?" Her voice feigned concern as she dramatically flourished the back of her hand to her forehead, "If I put them down here, I might break one of the broken pipes!" *CLUNK* the bags dropped and metal scraped underneath them before grinding to a halt, "I brought you Chinese takeout, so get your disgusting overalls over here and eat some before it gets cold." Esmeralda's gaze did not waver from her tinkering.

"I have to finish this." She said as the sister-in-law clicked her heels impatiently.

"I don't have all night, you have to eat." She sounded like an exacerbated mother attempting to get her toddler to eat vegetables.

"I did eat," Esmerelda responded, "I ate one of those canned soups you brought me." The other woman put her hands on her hips.

"And I'm sure that was a mere few hours ago right?" She raised her eyebrows awaiting a response. Esmeralda glanced at the bronze clock face laid out on workbench, and then continued to fiddle with her tiny wrench. "That's what I thought, you've been working on that one clock for so long, don't you look at it enough to have some sense of time?"

Esmeralda was finally satisfied with the movement of her hinge and set it down next to the clock face, only to pick up another oily piece of metal. The other woman was rapidly running out of patience and with a quick look at her own watch, decided she had enough. She stamped her foot to get Esmerelda's attention again.

"Get over here and eat!" She rustled around in one of the bags and pulled out a small white take out container with red lettering on the sides. "Don't make me come over there and take that grody thing away from you."

No response.

The woman took a few steps in Esmerelda's direction, carefully eyeing the floor for anything sharp. She saw mostly dirt, dirty paper and metal fragments, so rusted, that they were rapidly turning into dirt. She silently wished to herself that she wasn't wearing her new heels and attempted to step gracefully over a toppled and probably moldy car seat while still holding Esmerelda's dinner, but then her shoe caught on an indistinguishable piece of metal.

"Ack!" she cried out as she almost toppled into a rat's nest of sharp wires, but she put her hand on the corner of a table to brace herself just in time.

"Goodness! If this mess doesn't kill you, it'll kill me. You have got to clean up in here." She had used different words at one time or another. Sometimes she argued, sometimes she pleaded, sometimes she just hinted, but she had made the same statement for almost a decade. She looked down at the luckily mostly clear spot on the workbench corner where her hand had landed and saw the corner of a slip of paper that she recognized. She pulled out the yellowing card from under the pile of debris and frowned. It read:

You are cordially invited

to the wedding of

Jack Climpson and Kiki Elmsley

"Isn't that lovely. It's one of the many invitations I gave you for my wedding that you didn't attend," Kiki said. Esmeralda's tinkering halted for a moment and then she slumped a bit lower as Kiki managed to finally get her other leg over the dilapidated car seat. She stood there in the sea of odd bits and ends not quite knowing where to step next. So instead of trying to navigate the ocean of garbage she put the hand not holding hot takeout aggressively on her hip, "Are you done with that yet?"

"Almost," Esmeralda said, turning her head away from Kiki's glare.

"Well at least you are finally working on something other than that weird cuckoo clock."

"This is a part of the clock."

Kiki frowned and changed the subject back to her chief concern.

"It really looks like a category 5 hurricane meets a junkyard in here though, and we both know you are never going to use all these things. Jack and I will help you spruce things up a bit if you want."

Esmeralda said nothing. She didn't have to speak, she had already declined many times, but Kiki knew this was not like the other times.

"Our offer was accepted on that house today."

"Congratulations," Esmerelda said.

Kiki shifted uncomfortably and greasy papers rustled beneath her feet.

"It's super far across town though, I won't be able to come over and bug you as much and it's really not good for you to be in this absolute deathtrap of a house alone. I'd feel truckloads better if some truckloads of stuff left this house before I move." Kiki tried to smile but it was hard when it went unnoticed. "The house we put an offer in for has got this fabulous unfinished basement. It has a window so you could get in your vitamin D, 10-foot ceilings so it doesn't feel like a cave… and we'll have a spare bedroom! So, Jack and I talked it over and you are free to come live with us for a while if you want. You can even bring some of your stuff. Doesn't that sound great! We can set up a nice clean work area for you and…"

"No thanks." Esmerelda responded, expressionless.

Kiki took a deep breath through her clenched smile.

"Esmerelda, this house is going to fall down on top of you if this horde of junk doesn't first. Both Jack and I feel extraordinarily strongly that you should toss out most of this crummy stuff, sell the house that's crumbling down around you, and move in with us at our nice, clean, and much more structurally stable house for the time being."

Esmerelda's hands trembled as she fumbled with a tiny screwdriver, trying to process what this all meant, but Kiki couldn't take her silence anymore.

"Are you even listening to me!" Kiki shouted. Esmeralda dropped her screwdriver altogether. It clattered loudly to the floor, but she sat with her hand still hovering in the air for a moment, her fingers twitching ever so slightly.

"It's not just stuff," Esmerelda said, a trace of emotion evident in her voice, "It's Edward's stuff, it's Edward's house." Kiki's face softened, and she chose her words carefully.

"I know, and I know it's going to be hard. But I think this is the right way to go, for your wellbeing, and my sanity."

The familiar silence was as thick as the dust in the air as Esmerelda got down off her stool to try and retrieve the screwdriver from under the workbench. As she escaped out of sight Kiki tried to reassure her.

"I'm not saying you have to get rid of every last thing, even some of the things I think should be burned in dumpster fire I know are very important to you. So, we can put some of it in storage, and you can have some of it at the house."

Esmeralda reluctantly stood up from under the workbench and sat back down at her workstation before saying, "No."

Kiki's face turned red.

"What would he say if he saw you now, huh? He wouldn't want you to live like this Esmerelda!"

Esmeralda's only response was to hunch over and bury her face deeper in her work, trying desperately in her head to work out what she should say and then ultimately, saying nothing. But Kiki wasn't about to let her off another time.

"When will this get through your thick skull? I am trying to help you! I have done nothing but try to help you for years and what do I get? Nothing! I've always been nice to you ever since we met. Edward always said, "Oh, she's just shy. She's just not very good with people but she's really great," and out of love for my brother I tried to like you. I really did. I tried to reach out to you, but you never reached back. I know this was his house, I know these are his projects. Do you not think I get that? Long before he was your husband, he was my brother. I loved him first." Kiki slammed the takeout on the corner of the workbench and turned to leave. "You two were similar in a lot of ways, always tinkering and getting distracted. But you know the one big thing that set you two apart was that even though he had a lot of stuff, he never let that stuff get between him and his family." She took a deep breath and her tone softened. "I know that if he had a choice between all his stuff and the people he cared about, he wouldn't even hesitate. But you, you don't even care that I'm here. I come here almost every other day for years and you never even come for Christmas. In fact, you never come out of this house for anything, you didn't even come to my wedding! *My wedding*! You care more about that one stupid clock than me!"

"No… no I don't!" Esmeralda's eyes shot up to look at her and thoughts of a carefully planned sentence went out the window. "I thought you wanted this, he wanted this." Kiki's mascara was streaming down her face.

"Why on earth would I want to live like this? Why would I want you to live like this?" Esmeralda blinked. You could see gears turning behind the tears welling up in her eyes.

"I mean, I'm sorry um, Thank you… Your wedding, he, I…. don't know… what I'm supposed to say."

Esmerelda slumped down onto the workbench with her face in her arms and for a few moments the clock face ticking slowly, surrounded by clutter on the table, was the only sound echoing off the walls. Then with her head still in the crook of her arm she felt around under the workbench and pulled out a drawer. Her muffled voice came from the table.

"It was supposed to be a surprise." She felt around in the drawer, pulled out a folder, and set it on the table. Its smudged but bright pink cover contrasted with the gray and brown hues of everything around it. She recognized her brother's handwriting labeling it:

Kiki's Special Project

Esmeralda's face was still buried in the table with no sign of motion or explanation. So Kiki carefully made her way toward the workbench, picked up the folder, and gingerly opened it. It was plans and drawings for a clock. Except this cuckoo clock had quite the whimsical design. The cuckoo clock was a wonky looking bird with a bronze clock set in its chest. Blue wings carved from wood were supposed to flap up and down on the hour and a long purple tongue stuck out as the clock cooed. The most recent blueprint was from 5 years ago, but as she flipped through the pages, she quickly realized that this had been an ongoing project. She found blueprints and drawings dating back ten, fifteen, and nearly twenty years ago.

As Kiki thumbed through all the pages of blueprints and brainstorming, she found that in the back there was one page with a page protector over it. She carefully pulled it out and blinked in surprise. It was a drawing of the clock, but not a polished engineering blueprint or an artist's final concept. It was the drawing of a child. A drawing of a cuckoo clock with blue wings, a pink body and a floppy polka dot hat. Across the bottom in large letters from a hand that had just learned to spell:

Kiki

A faint memory crossed her mind of smiles and pride when this picture was displayed proudly on the fridge for a couple of years. Esmeralda finally looked up.

"He said you were so happy when you drew that and he wanted to bring it to life for his little sister. He always said he was going to finish it. First it was Christmas, then it was your birthday, then the birthday after that. It gave him so much trouble and he got so busy it kept getting pushed back. The same thing happened to me. I tried to finish it for your wedding present. I thought I could finish it at least mostly if I worked down to the wire. But by the time I realized I wouldn't be able to show up with anything presentable, I had lost track of time and your wedding had already started. I was still going to rush over and come but then I realized I wouldn't have a gift, and that you wouldn't like anything I had to wear, and then I thought you probably just invited me because you had to and didn't want me to come anyway." There was a pause, "You've done so much for me I thought this was something I could do for you. I know you don't like me. I don't know how to fix that. But I do know how to fix stuff. I know how to fix this. I thought if I finished this clock that would make him happy. I thought it would make you happy." Esmeralda stood and looked at Kiki. "I guess I'll eat now. Thanks for bringing me food, again. She reached for the carton in Kiki's hand."

"Wait," Kiki pulled it away and Esmeralda looked at her with big green eyes, wondering if she had said something disastrously wrong.

"It… it would make me very happy if you finished the clock. But it would make me happier if you took better care of yourself and I knew you were safe." Esmerelda relaxed.

"Ok," said Esmerelda. Kiki took a deep breath.

"So will you let me help you? Please, for both of us and for Edward." Esmeralda hesitated, but only for a moment.

"Yeah, thank you."

"You're welcome," Kiki gave her the warm box, nimbly stepped back over the chair, and fished around in the plastic bags once more, "I've got one too. You want to chow down together?"

"Sure," Esmerelda's eyes darted around the room, flitting from one pile to another, "I guess there isn't a place for two to sit in here."

"Yes, not without a bit of work," Kiki sighed. Esmeralda shifted a bit uncomfortably.

"Well, I guess we could go outside on the front porch and eat," she said looking down at the stain covered floor.

"If you're ok with that," said Kiki.

"Yeah, I'm ok with that."

So, the two of them carefully made their way single file up the creaking stairs out of the basement. In the fading light they stumbled through a narrow pathway lined with newspapers and boxes leading to the front door. Once outside in the twilight of evening, they plopped down on the cool concrete porch steps and looked out over a dim empty street. A single streetlamp illuminated their view as they unboxed their dinners and broke open their chopsticks. Then they shoveled takeout unceremoniously down their throats, watching the sun set and the moon rise.

Voids

Apoorva Batra

At times,
The voids I carry within my heart, ache,
Ache bad. Oh! I burn within,
All I can do is cry.

Reminding me of my wounds, old and new,
At the darkest of dark,
My voids sting like never before,
These voids are carved by my soul scars,

After a point,
I started questioning myself
What have I done to deserve these voids,
My soul searches for an answer but fails to find one.

These voids are searching for love to be filled with,
These voids are yearning to be touched by the flawless
beauty of another soul,
These voids of mine want sunflowers to
grow within and bloom.

Lost

Apoorva Batra

I'm lost between my identity and my reflection,
When I look into the mirror,
I saw pieces of melted words stick on my lips,
I woke up to this dirty face,
last night,
When I was trying to write a poem,
I was struggling with words, thoughts and feelings,
When my words started melting in fire of their own,
Some meaningless, distorted words stuck at corner of my lips,
When I woke up,
I even tried to trace those left pieces of residual words from my lips,
but,

But didn't find any poem.

I only found my pen, crumbled papers of my diary and silence surrounded with an unknown fear of being lost.

Sancity Of Love

Apoorva Batra

Never have I touched you,

Never have I kissed you,

Never have I held you in my arms,

Never have I held your hands, and felt your touch

But baby,

I'm so fortunate and blessed

To have your pure love which is beyond

any touch,

any kiss

And you know I'm holding your heart

As much as you hold mine with all the sanctity.

Purpose

Sanjana Chhatlani

As I lit the pyre, a whole gamut of emotions overcame me. Guilt ripped my heart, thinking of the umpteen options I could have tried rather than letting go. That disdainful feeling engulfed me bit by bit as lit the fire, the pyre.

Whatever the last decision, why does it always feel so wrong? The ifs and buts poked their ugly head again, robbing me of the minuscule composure I would force upon myself from time to time.

I watched the larger-than-life, loud, gregarious, and strong person turn to dust before me. How can one ever overcome such a loss? The silence such people leave behind can be deafening. I couldn't see the suffering. I didn't want him to suffer either.

Why couldn't things happen my way? Why couldn't he just get well and get back to normal life?

His absence; the void he left behind, stood like a gaping hole in the center of my heart. It would take years of distractions and newer experiences if I even hoped to cover it superficially.

The whole rigmarole in hospital, the drips, the injections, the operation theatre, the flustered doctors, the beeps of the monitors policing his rebellious heartbeat, oxygen saturation, BP, and some other parameters, everything flashed before my eyes, making me touch new lows every time.

Why couldn't I just turn the whole thing around? Why couldn't I just move back in time a little and erase this event from my life?

I couldn't find shelter from my thoughts and they threatened to overpower me and then destroy me completely, just like the virus did to him. For three days, I spoke to so many people who offered me condolences, lent an ear to my woes, wished me strength, and expressed their grief either in their equation with him or by way of some other random event of their life. But the scenes from the hospital and his helpless face kept coming back to haunt me.

The ashes still had his essence, and I thought how our rituals emphasized letting go again and again. I'd have to release the ashes as well. On day five, I reached the Kund. I sat at the steps, clinging on to the last of his remains. I feared, letting go of them would steal him from me completely. How would I face life now, all by myself, without the protection I took so much for granted? Maybe I could drown with them.

A little boy, about 10 years old, came by and asked, 'Sir, can I immerse them for you, I will take the ashes right to the center of the Kund for you. Only Rs.50.'

I looked at him, utterly shocked. The Kund had so many visitors every day, immersing ashes in it. How and why would this little boy jump into it?

'Why should you do that? Where are your parents? Do they know you are doing ridiculous things here? Are you trying to earn a fast buck? What do you want to do with the money?'

The little boy didn't even look alarmed. He looked at me with cold eyes and said,

'Why are you screaming? If you don't want my service, just say so. This is my job. I make anywhere between 300 to 400 rupees every day. What's your problem?'

I felt overwhelmed. I spoke a little more gently.

'Oh gosh! Are your parents aware that you are doing this work?' Have they sent you to do this work?' I was already thinking of a hundred possibilities. But he said,

'I don't have parents, Sir. I'm an orphan. They say my mother died while giving birth to me and my father died of alcohol abuse soon after. We are about 8 – 10 orphans, staying with Girish Bhai. Each one of us needs to take up some or the other random job around here. If we manage to make around 300 each, then we hand most of the money to him. In return he lets us stay with him and provides food.'

I felt numbed. No father? No mother? No childhood? No pampering, cajoling, fun and laughter, festivals, celebrations, happy bonding, studying, fighting, tantrums, love, and affection? The child probably didn't even know he was missing something. Or maybe he did.

God! So this was his level of acceptance of his circumstances. Shivers ran down my spine. Fear? He probably didn't know what fear was. Or fear to him meant not being able to earn or having to go without food. I felt petty. If losing my parent at a ripe old age made me insecure, what was this child going through?

I couldn't get myself to say anything more or ask anything more to him. I just nodded, telling him that I didn't need his service.

He tried to pester me a little, hoping that I would give in. But I couldn't imagine him diving into that pond and I just turned him away. But he stood where he was.

I looked at the ashes in my hand. None of the pain I had been experiencing for the past so many days surfaced. Suddenly, all the suffering that I had been going through felt like a distant blur. Dad had gone. He had suffered undoubtedly, but his body gave up at one point and he was relieved, released from that pain and suffering. But I was still dwelling in that suffering and experiencing his pain even though it no longer existed. He had freed himself from the shackles of physical suffering and I needed to release myself from the shackles of mental and emotional suffering. I didn't need to punish myself for his suffering and continue it mentally. This was truly what letting go was all about.

I quietly released the ashes into the water. I saw them blend and become one with the water. Rituals are not about anything. Dad had become one with the mighty force. It felt like releasing his spirit and it blended into nature. I suddenly began to feel his presence all around me. In the air, in the trees, in the water … I couldn't see him, but I could sense him. There was never going to be a physical form to reach out to. I understood the difference between a person dying and a person ceasing to exist. Dad didn't cease to exist, he just changed into an unknown form. My eyes turned moist again.

That boy just stood and watched me. He said nothing. I wondered what he was thinking. Was he able to understand my loss, my pain? Was he able to understand what I felt? Or did he just watch me, thinking about his loss of business, and curse me? I offered the little boy a hundred bucks, nonetheless, in Dad's name. He pursed his lips but said nothing. I gestured again for him to come and take it. A hundred bucks meant a lot to him and he came and took it from me.

He said,'You gave me the money for free, without taking my service…'

'It's ok. My Dad would have wanted me to give it to you. Keep it. You need it', I said, smiling lightly. He left. So much self-esteem! The work didn't matter. He was happy earning it. Amazing! Life taught hard lessons.

I waited for a while, and my thoughts went back to my Dad, reminiscing the happy moments we shared, some odd jokes that would never be part of my life again. I didn't feel like leaving. Going back to an empty house felt horrible. I'd have to work out the purpose of my life all over again. One, that didn't feature him anymore. Our lives had been entwined in each other's for so long now, I could think of anything without him. I felt miserable again. Is it possible to live with the essence of a person? With memories? The nightmare I dreaded the most for so many years, had finally come true. Dad was gone. It felt like standing in waist-deep water in the sea, prepared for the wave to come and hit, but being uprooted and thrown back by the force. Death is the ultimate truth no one can escape or shy away from. The absence of the loved one is the part that's most difficult to cope with.

I was lost in my thoughts when another family came to immerse the ashes of a family member in the Kund. The little boy offered his services to them and they agreed. I watched aghast as the boy, without any hint of hesitation, aversion, or fear just dived into the pond where I had released Dad's ashes minutes ago. I felt nauseous. He took the ashes and swam to the center of the pool, disappeared for a bit, and then swam back empty-handed to collect his fee. It all happened so fast. I wanted to call out to him and stop him. I wanted to tell the family, not to send the boy in, but I froze. What right did I have to take away his livelihood, anyway? What was I expecting? Giving him a hundred bucks would sort his problem for life? The extra hundred was probably just a lucky bonus for him.

The family left. I kept watching him. He was all wet. He sat to soak in the beating afternoon sun. He didn't even bother to change or dry himself. He was more concerned about counting and keeping his earnings safe. He saw me looking at him and asked,

'You haven't left?'

I just smiled. At least I had beautiful memories to cherish. Oh, I had a treasure-trove of wonderful memories that I could bring back at will and relive. What about this kid? No memories to fall back on. I asked him, 'Is this your only method of earning? You could do something else… sweeping, cleaning, etc. Why this work?'

I did clean and sweep in someone's house before. But a theft took place and I was blamed for it. I am not a thief sir; I am telling you the truth. I didn't steal. But they beat me and threw me out of the job. I tried ironing. But I burnt one cloth and the owner of the laundry fired me. This work is good, Sir. I am on my own. I don't have to answer anyone. I never run out of work. I make money every day.' My head was reeling. But I wanted to know more.

'So once you call it a day here, what do you do then?'

Oh, in the evening? Yeah, once I am done here, I go back to our room in the Chawl, clean the utensils, wash my clothes and then head to the market to buy stuff for cooking our meal at night.'

My heart lost a beat. He probably didn't know the meaning of playing or hobbies. For him unwinding from the day's work was only more work. Different work.

'In the past two years, what was the thing that made you happy? What activity did you do that made you happy?'

He thought long and hard but stayed silent.

'Come on. Tell me! It could be anything. Maybe some game, some fun, something?'

'Oh yes, fun! We do a lot of fun. Sometimes when Girish Bhai goes to the city far away, we all put on music and dance a lot. Dagdu, my friend, arranges everything for us. That is a lot of fun. Once, at the junction around the corner, the man selling fritters and other yum snacks on his mobile stand left it unmanned for 2 minutes, Dagdu wheeled the entire stand into our room. Oh, what fun we had. We ate up all the snacks to our heart's content.'

'Weren't you all caught?' I asked, curious.

'Of course, we were caught. Everyone had seen Dagdu with the mobile stand. The man who owned the stand and Girish Bhai, both beat us. Dagdu was beaten with a bat. But at the end of the day, we had that little adventure and so much fun.'

I heaved a sigh. I didn't know what to tell him. Preaching would have been such an easy option and I was brimming. But he didn't need it. He wouldn't understand. He lived such a deprived life that he wouldn't understand. If beating didn't help, mere words absolutely wouldn't. I asked instead,

'Did you ever go to school? Do you know how to read or write? Have you given a thought to what you would want to be when you grow up?'

Oh, I never went to school. I can't read or write. But I know that when I grow up I want to be like Dagdu. He is so smart and clever!' he replied with sheer admiration and awe for his idol.

I was shocked. He was so deprived but had such deep acceptance of his circumstances that he didn't even dare to dream beyond his limited life. That was it. I turned towards him and asked earnestly,

'Will you come with me? You will have to stay in a hostel and go to school every day. You will have to study every day. All this work will need to be stopped. Is that ok with you?'

He looked at me with doubt and disbelief.

'How can I stop working? What will I eat if I don't earn?' He asked matter-of-factly.

'Oh; the hostel will provide you with food…All three meals. But you will have to be on your best behavior. You will have to study hard. It will be tough. Want to do it?' He didn't seem convinced.

'Why should I trust you? What if you cut my hands or feet or scoop out my eyes and then make me beg at the signal? That is what happened with Rolu.'

'Ok, if I take Girish Bhai with me to the hostel and get your admission done, then will it be ok? Will you trust me if Girish Bhai vouches for me?'

He thought for a while and nodded. But then immediately said,'But there are more boys here with me. Mattu, Teeku, Jeetu, Vagya ..'

I smiled. In absence of family, they were all his family. And it was natural to be concerned about their well-being.

I thought for a while and said,'Ok, let's try this. You will be the first one to be put in a hostel. You don't have to do anything there but attend school and study. Food provided. If you do well in six months, that is if you study properly, then we will bring Mattu too. If Mattu works hard with his studies then after six months we will put Teeku. Is that fine? You will need to prove yourselves. I need to see if you are happy being educated or you'd rather do all that work, earn and provide for yourself. If you don't perform, then I will bring you back here to lead the life you have been leading so far. The choice is yours. Take a call.'

For the first time, I saw a twinkle in his eyes. They were twinkling with hope. Hope of a life beyond the Kund, that he had not even imagined so far. He looked at the Kund. He turned back to me and nodded. I looked at the Kund too. Dad had seen to it that I was not going back empty. I nodded and smiled too. Together, we climbed up the stairs, leaving the Kund behind. He, for a better life and me, with a new sense of purpose!

Cougar

Pooja Natoo

Too close, too much
I've held fire in my heart
Warmth so ravenous
It's all black deadbeat now
I feel no remorse
Life is but a set of wrongly joint pages
And yet we found each other
A tumble down the streets
Photographs and paradoxes
Intensity so phenomenal
My legs are weak with the weight of it

Great love, they said,

'A heart with no brain'

It's an abyss

Seized by hands

Conquering hands,

Hands that lack softness

And rhythm

And yet and yet and yet

I jump off the rooftop

I dive into the lagoon

I walk threadbare

The madness runs in my veins

My mother said,

'Emotions are best kept compartmentalized'

Fear and love hitch a ride together

Misery oversees it all

It's a jumbled mess

I misplaced the labels on

Love and Dependence

Dark and light,

My dependence is dead poets

And late night revelations on year old chat

It is making moulds of clays

And going through them with a sledgehammer

Love is an overused tissue

Lying on the grey asphalt

We walk over it all the time

And never ever realise
The beauty lies in the unknown
You walk backwards now,
Love last or a passing stop?
Surprised
Stars and lovers
White sheets and daring breaths
It all comes together
A little bit of compliance
A lot more of push
The end is near
Sadness claws my throat
Tequila shuts it out
A curving hill
And destination unknown
Flip through
The stack of cassettes
Ask me, 'Which story shall I chose today?'

Eclipse

George Styles

When I get up in the morning, I do a quick hygiene check, and then, without breakfast, I head down to my basement to my exercise equipment. I start on the heavy bag, slowly punching until I feel myself begin to wake up, and then I work away for about ten to fifteen minutes. After this, I head over to the weights and do some lifting till I am sufficiently hungry for breakfast. And at that point, I grab breakfast. I do this mainly because exercise gets me what I want, and that is to stay fit. But the other reason I do this is that I have been doing this for a while now. Since grade four, I have been working away with weights. And now, with my last year of elementary school coming up, it's a permanent habit.

However, on this particular day, I received a knock at the door while I was in the middle of breakfast. I went to the door to find my friend, Ed, smiling away. I motioned him to come in and offered him some breakfast.

"So, what's going on today?" Ed asked, eating away at his bowl of cereal.

"I haven't figured that out yet," I replied.

"Well," Ed continued.

"You should come down to the docks with me,"

"I'm going to meet up with this hot chic."

"Hot chic?" I said, smirking.

"Oh fuck yeah, buddy!" Ed smiled.

"Erin is hot!"

I laughed and shook my head. Ed then continued.

"Well," he began.

"I'm also going to be checking out who is hanging out at the docks."

"So what are you saying, buddy,"

"You down?"

Figuring that Ed didn't want to tell me straight up that he needed a wingman to hook up with this girl, I quickly obliged. With the end of our breakfast, we decided to start walking the long walk to the docks. We soon got out of our neighborhood and decided to take a path through a field which shortened the journey.

"Fuck, it's bright out," Ed said as we walked down the path.

"I think I already got a tan just from being out here for five minutes."

"Yeah," I replied, noting that it was a bright day.

"Would have been nice to have some sunglasses."

"Fuck ya, buddy," Ed smiled.

"We should go jack some from the store."

"Oh no," I laughed.

"Besides,"

"Don't they only have the ones that all the old people wear?"

"For sure," Ed laughed.

"But we could always stop in at the mall."

"I'm good," I laughed.

"Yeah, man," Ed agreed.

"That's too much walking."

We got through the field and then took another trail to an obscure street that led to a parking lot. After getting through the parking lot, we quickly took a road that directly led to the area near the docks. As we passed a convenience store, a few guys standing outside sitting on their bikes called us over.

"Hey Ed!" one of them yelled.

"Oh, hey!" Ed replied to him, motioning me to follow him.

We walked up to the smiling crew outside the convenience store.

"What's going on, Ed?" the guy said, reaching his hand out.

"Heading to the docks," Ed replied, shaking his hand.

"What about you guys?"

The whole crew began snickering away, turning their heads to some smiling kid in the convenience store, who looked to be searching for something in the candy aisle.

"We're waiting for Franky to jack some shit," one of them snickered away.

Ed and I looked over at the scene going on inside.

"Ha!" Ed laughed.

'Look at the clerk at the counter!"

The clerk watched on all while Franky took his time, looking at the candy choices far too long not to be suspicious. The clerk, of course, who also noticed our presence, had a full smirk on his face as, in this town, everyone knew what was coming. We continued to talk to the crew, who then went on to tell us about some theft-spree they had gone on at the mall. As they spoke away, the convenience store doors suddenly burst open, with Franky holding a double armful of goods, screaming for everyone to get out of there. The crew then took off instantly, with the clerk emerging from the store, running right after them. Ed laughed away at the scene as I watched on, wondering if they were going to get away. As it turned out, the clerk hadn't responded fast enough. This lack of response from the clerk gave the crew enough time to get a head start, with one even having enough time to stop and pick up Franky and their heist goods. They all rode off, giving the clerk the finger all while yelling all sorts of obscenities. The clerk screamed a few of his own and then turned and began walking back to the store. Ed and I took this as our cue to get out of there.

"Ha, fucking cashier bitch," Ed laughed as we started walking away.

"Anyway, bud,"

"Erin just lives five doors down."

We walked on to a duplex where Ed jogged ahead of me, ran up the steps, and knocked on the door. After a few seconds, a girl came to the door, opening it and immediately smiling and hugging Ed.

"Erin," Ed began, turning around to look at me at the bottom of the steps.

"This is my buddy, Derek."

The girl turned and immediately smiled and came down the steps and gave me a greeting hug.

"Hi Derek," she said.

"Great to meet you," I replied.

After the greeting, we walked up to her veranda. Then, I looked over to Ed, who seemed to be looking at me as if I should keep talking. I quickly shot him a look back to tell him that I had nothing to say.

"Yeah, so Erin," Ed began.

"What's happening today?"

"I'm just babysitting my little brother and sister," she replied.

"Oh, cool," Ed replied, looking over at me.

"Sounds like fun."

As Ed continued with the small talk, I stood there, watching like some awkward third wheel. However, I couldn't help but notice something. It was strange. The girl herself did not look like she was from our town. Indeed, she had a sort of innocence and kindness that didn't seem typical of the rest of us. She appeared nonjudgmental and was friendly in a way that wasn't typical of our particular town. She didn't fit in but in a good way. As I stood there thinking away, I was then suddenly broken out of my trance.

"You're not in a relationship?" Erin asked me, catching me completely off-guard.

"Huh?" I replied, lost from the conversation.

"Ed says you don't have a girlfriend?" she asked again.

"Oh," I began.

"No, no, I don't," I said, all while Ed made faces and kept lip-synching something that I couldn't quite decipher. Finally, after seeing I wasn't getting what he was saying, he then spoke.

"Hey, listen, Erin," Ed said, smirking on at me.

"I'll be right back in a minute."

"Would you mind looking after Derek here for a minute or two?"

Just as I was about to protest, Ed then jumped off the veranda and began jogging away.

"I'll be right back!" he hollered as he ran off.

"I uh," I began as I watched him speed away.

"I can just go," I said, motioning that I could just leave and get out of there.

"No, it's okay!" Erin replied, smiling.

"We just met!"

After a few awkward moments of talk, my bout of imposter syndrome began to wear off. As I continued to reply to all her questions, I finally decided to ask a few things about her.

"So," I began.

"You got a boyfriend?"

As soon as I finished the very last word, her face lit up, but strangely, she didn't smile.

"Yes," she said.

"And he's older than me."

"Oh?" I replied.

"How, much older?"

"He's twenty," she replied.

Immediately, I felt myself come to a complete internal stop.

"Twenty?" I gasped, thinking I had misheard what she said.

"Yes, twenty," she replied.

I looked on. This girl couldn't have been older than me. Despite my internal discombobulation, I pushed to make it look like what I had just heard had no effect.

"Oh, that's cool," I said, pushing off my cognitive delirium.

"So, is he at work?" I asked, now wondering if this was his house.

"Well," Erin began.

"He's in jail right now,"

"But he'll be getting out next month."

I stood there, now with my brain screaming away, fighting hard to push out a quick reply, but trying hard not to reveal what was going on in my head.

"Next month?" I asked.

"Yeah," she replied.

"He's my baby's father."

I kept trying my very hardest to look on at her as if she had just given me a recipe for cherry pie. Finally, I nodded to conceal my inner turmoil.

"Oh, you have a baby?" I said, thinking this was getting crazier and crazier by the moment.

"Yes, I'm three months along," she replied, looking down at her stomach.

"Doesn't look like it, huh?"

I forced out a smile and nodded away.

"No, not at all," I replied.

"You had me fooled."

Erin started to laugh away, smiling on at me. Just then, and in perfect timing, Ed then showed up.

"Hey, hey!" he said as he walked up to her veranda.

"What's going on?"

"Just talking," I replied, nodding and smiling.

"Okay," Ed began.

"Listen, Erin,"

"We're gonna head over to the docks now,"

"I guess we'll catch you later."

"Where did you go?" I asked, looking at Ed as if he was crazy. We both continued to walk down the street towards the docks with an odd, fast pace.

"Check it out," Ed said, waving a pack of cigarettes in front of my face.

"Shit, man, why didn't you just take me with you?" I said, thinking about how Ed had just taken off without prior warning.

"Ha, buddy!" Ed laughed, holding a devious smile on his face. I shook my head.

"So, do you know the dude she's with?" I asked, seeing if Ed had any insights.

"Ha!" Ed began.

"He's a fuckin' joker."

"Buddy goes around saying he's in for armed robbery."

"But really, he got caught stealing furniture from an old folk's home."

I looked over at Ed.

"He did that?" I gasped.

"You know it, bud," Ed snickered.

"That's insane," I replied.

"But Erin seems like a nice girl, though."

"Ha," Ed laughed.

"Yeah, but you know this town, bud."

"The biggest douchebags get all the talent."

I walked on as I had no reply. All I could think about was whether Erin was even aware of her situation. With my head spinning away, we walked onwards to the docks.

Once we got there, some guy immediately walked up to us. Ed quickly nudged me and began snickering.

"Ha!" he laughed away in a hushed voice.

"Buddy's name is Chris."

"Cool," I replied.

Chris continued to walk right on up to us as if he was the owner of the docks himself.

"Hey, Chris," Ed said, smiling.

"What's going on?"

"Uh, today, it's my birthday," Chris replied.

"Oh shit, man, Happy Birthday!" Ed said, smiling and reaching his hand over to Chris.

"Yeah," Chris continued, shaking Ed's hand.

"So I'll be having a party later."

"It's bring your own booze."

"Bring your own booze?" Ed replied, looking on at Chris as if he had said something weird.

"That's what I said," Chris replied.

"Okay," Ed laughed.

"But how are we gonna get our own booze?"

"You'll think of something," Chris said, looking at Ed as if he was stupid.

Ed smiled and nodded. After giving me a look that this Chris guy was a bit out of it, we then walked on to see who else was hanging around. As we walked on, we noticed a crew all hanging out ahead of us.

"Nice fucking shirt," Ed laughed at some kid, who turned and smiled.

"Eddy!" he laughed, turning around to high-five him.

"Long time no see, man!"

"Mark," Ed began turning to me.

"This is my buddy, Derek."

Mark looked at me and smiled.

"Hey man, nice to meet you," he said, extending his hand.

"You too, Mark," I replied, shaking his hand.

"So what brings you lads down here today?"

Ed began to tell Mark how we had just got down here and how the Chris guy had walked right up to us, telling us it was his birthday. As Ed disclosed the brief encounter, Mark began to shake his head back and forth.

"Man," Mark began.

"That guy is a clown," he explained.

"Get this guy,"

"We all come down here,"

"And he's going on about how it's his birthday."

"And like,"

"That's cool and all."

"So we wish him happy birthday, and he then starts telling us about his party."

"So, at that point, he's got our attention."

"But then he tells us it's bring your own booze."

"And we're all like, what the fuck?"

"Fucking buddy!" Ed laughed, pointing over at Chris, who looked to be talking with a crowd of people.

"Yeah, man," Mark confirmed.

"He's a total clown."

"Ha!" Ed laughed while still looking over at the crowd.

"Like, how does he expect anyone to get booze?"

"None of us look old enough."

"What a fucking clown!" Ed laughed again.

"So anyway," Mark began.

"We just came down here to see what's up."

"And if anyone had smokes."

"Oh," Ed began.

"You want a smoke?"

Ed reached into his pocket and pulled out his pack, and presented Mark with a cigarette.

"Oh shit yeah, man," Mark said, taking the cigarette from Ed.

"I haven't scored all day."

"Thanks a lot, man," he said, lighting up and taking a drag, exhaling away in the air.

As Mark smoked away, we noticed that the rest of the crowd suddenly turned and immediately walked over.

"Marky!" one of them yelled out as he made his way over.

"Gimme a drag!"

"Sure, man," Mark said as he quickly flashed his eyes at Ed, signaling him to hide his cigarette pack.

"Marky!" another yelled out.

"Gimme a drag, buddy."

"Fuckin' vultures," Mark said in a hushed voice as now all the crowd was standing where we were. I looked over and noticed that Chris was standing all alone. He and his birthday were not as entertaining as a single cigarette. After realizing his sudden drop in popularity, he slowly began to walk over to where everyone was.

"Yo, buddy," one of Mark's crew yelled over to Ed.

"You got any more smokes, bud?"

Immediately, Mark shot Ed a quick look that surely spoke volumes about staying quiet about his cigarettes.

"Ah," Ed replied, looking kind of caught with the whole situation.

"Well, I can give you guys three,"

"Cause, this pack has got to last me."

"Oh fuck yeah, man!" one of the crew said.

Ed then opened up his pack and took out three cigarettes. He then handed them over to one of the crew.

"Well," the guy said.

"I know what I'm smoking."

The guy smirked away, turning away from the others, who now looked completely rattled.

"Andrew!" one of them yelled.

"Fuck you, man!"

"Sucks to lose," Andrew replied, walking over to the side with all three cigarettes.

The others started to beg him to share. Andrew ignored them and then lit one of the cigarettes up. He then blew the smoke in all their faces.

"You're all a bunch of slow-ass bitches," he laughed as the others watched on.

Finally, after some minutes of watching as he smoked away, the others then turned back to Ed.

"Listen, man," one of them said, walking up to Ed.

"I hate to ask,"

"But is it possible you can give us a smoke?"

"Just one,"

"We'll share it."

Mark again shot Ed a look. Again, Ed looked back at Mark.

"Okay, man," Ed said, pulling out his cigarette pack.

Just as he was about to open it, the guy then snatched the whole pack and took off, running much faster than anyone could register. Now, they all ran off to catch up to the guy who had snatched the cigarette pack. Even Andrew had run off with them, suggesting that all of it had just been a plan all along. Mark then sat there staring at Ed.

"Ed," he began.

"I told you not to."

"Motherfuckers!" Ed hollered out, still standing where we were as the crew ran off down the street, not looking back.

"Fucking fucks!" Ed yelled off to them as they disappeared off in the distance.

"Fuck!"

"Listen, man," Mark began.

"I can go try and pinch some smokes for you if you want," he said, looking over at me.

"Ed," I began.

"Why don't we just chase them down?"

"Ah fuck," Ed began, looking disappointed.

"They're all long fucking gone now."

"Ed," Mark said, looking back at me.

"The three of us could kick their asses and get your smokes back."

"What do you say?"

"You got punked pretty hard there," Chris said, as he had been standing there the whole time.

"Eat a dick, Chris, you motherfucker!" Ed snapped back.

"Why didn't you stop them?"

Chris looked on at Ed as if he hadn't said anything.

"I was gonna ask you for a smoke."

"Well, go get them ya fuckin' dick," Ed said, pacing around, frustrated.

"There's your birthday present!"

"Ya fucking clown."

"What the fuck did you just say?" Chris snapped up, moving forward. Now I got ready. Although far bigger than all three of us, Chris hadn't been a help whatsoever.

"Back the fuck up," Mark said, stepping in front of Chris.

"Well, why are you guys blaming me?" Chris said, holding his arms up.

"They ran too fucking fast for me to do anything."

"Yeah, buddy," Ed said, shaking his head.

"If you hadn't been jerking yourself off the whole time,"

"Maybe you could have grabbed one of them!"

"What a fuckin' idea, huh?"

"Hey Eddie-" Chris said, now looking as if he was going to get up in Ed's face.

"Hey, you ugly dicks!" a voice shouted out from behind us. We all turned to see it was a few other people that usually hung out around the docks.

"You guys all whining about smokes?" one of them asked.

"Yeah," Ed began.

"Chris needs a smoke so he'll stop jerking himself off for his birthday."

"Hey!" Chris snapped over to Ed.

"Watch it!"

"You watch it!" Ed snapped back.

"Cool it," one of the people said. They then opened up their cigarette pack, took out two, and then passed the pack over to Ed.

"Now," the guy began.

"Try to share these."

"Oh fuck!" Ed gasped, looking into the cigarette pack.

"Thanks a lot, man!"

Just as everyone began to light up and talk away, I was hit with something unexpected.

"Derek!"

I turned around. For a moment, I was not able to register the face.

"I haven't seen you in like, forever!"

This girl, Jane, I had hung out with for the entire previous summer. But, for some reason, as soon as school kicked in, it was like that whole last summer had never happened.

"Hey," I said, smiling and putting my hand out to greet her.

She walked right on past my hand, jumped up, and gave me a great big hug.

"Wow, this is cool seeing you here," she said, jumping back down from almost smothering me.

"Yeah, how have you been?" I asked, catching my breath back from her attack.

"Not bad," she began.

"But we moved."

"So, I live like a few streets over from here-"

"So," a voice said, coming straight from out of nowhere.

"The party is over here."

I took a moment and then turned to him.

"Oh," I began.

"That's great, man," I said, kind of caught off-guard with his odd timing.

"I thought you were busy smoking."

"I was," Chris replied.

"But now I'm gonna talk to my friend, Jane."

"Uh," Jane said, turning from a smile to a straight look.

"Chris,"

"I haven't seen Derek in like a whole year,"

"So,"

"Don't fucking spoil it on me, please?"

"Uh, well," Chris began, looking surprised.

"I was just trying to tell you that it was my birthday and that I'm having a party tonight."

"And it's bring your own booze,"

"But I can get booze for you."

"Oh really?" Jane replied, not looking enthused.

"Well,"

"Happy Birthday, and that's great."

"But give me a few minutes to catch up with Derek, okay?"

"Oh yeah, yeah, for sure!" Chris said, then backing off and moving to join the others.

"So, as I was saying," Jane continued.

"I moved close to here,"

"And we moved right in September last year."

"But I'm sorry cause I should have called and told you!"

"It's cool," I said, thinking that it all seemed like it was yesterday.

"At least you're here right now."

"Yeah!" she said, jumping back to hug me again.

After a lengthy catch-up talk with Jane, all while continually getting interrupted by Chris, Ed approached me and pulled me aside.

"Listen, man," he said in a hushed voice, looking back to see if Chris was anywhere around.

"We're gonna take off on that fucking dick," he said, looking over to Chris, who was now stitched to Jane, who continued to look over to Ed and me as if to give us a sort of S.O.S. Ed then looked over to Mark, who was still talking with the crew of people who had been the evening's cigarette angels. Mark looked over quickly, shooting Ed a look that he was ready.

"But I'm hanging out with Derek tonight!" Jane said as she suddenly walked over and stood right beside me. Chris then walked right up to me, Ed and Jane.

"So," he began, staring at me.

"Are you guys coming to my party or what?" he asked in a not-so-friendly tone.

"Oh yeah, sure," Ed replied, smirking and shooting looks over to Mark.

"Can't fuckin' wait, buddy!"

"Okay, good," Chris replied, continuing to stare at me as Jane then moved to stand right beside me.

"So, Jane," he began.

"Why are you all over this guy?"

"Uh, excuse me?" Jane said, looking surprised.

"Uh, he's my fucking friend,"

"Maybe that's why?"

"Well, buddy," Chris said, moving towards me so as if to intimidate me.

"Why don't you-"

"RUN!" Ed yelled as he and Mark began to dash off. Just as I was about to throw in my part in the whole ordeal, Jane grabbed me by the arm, and soon, all four of us were racing away, looking back to see Chris, the birthday boy, just standing there, staring on at us as we ran off.

"What a fucking clown!" Ed laughed as we all slowed up to a stop. We all stood around trying to catch our breath while we laughed away at our sudden departure.

"That fucking guy is a serious dick," Mark added.

"Like I'm gonna party with that fucking loser."

"Yeah," Ed laughed.

"Bring my own booze,"

"More like suck my dick, buddy!"

"You didn't expect me to grab you to run," Jane said, smirking at me.

"No, not at all," I said, in agreement with her sudden move.

"I was thinking I was gonna get into a fight with that guy."

"Pfffff," Ed laughed.

"He's a fucking pussy!"

"Yeah, he's a total pussy," Mark agreed, shaking his head.

We all walked up the darkening street as we had agreed to walk Jane home. We continued talking about the whole incident, laughing away and being the loudest thing in the entire city block.

"Hey, guys!" Jane suddenly called out.

"My parents are gone tonight."

"They won't be back till midnight."

"Let's have a few drinks!"

"Whoa!" Mark spoke up.

"You know where they keep their alcohol?"

"Of course!" Jane laughed.

"And they don't keep track of it!"

"Oh yeah!" Ed yelled out down the street.

"Let's drink!"

We continued walking on, laughing and ready to raid Jane's parent's liquor stock. As we continued to yell and laugh away, we noticed that up ahead of us some distance was a large group of people heading our way. Immediately, Mark and Ed brought their volume down and began to look ahead at the crowd walking towards us. As our group got closer and closer, we could see that they were bigger than us, and they looked way older. Finally, as both groups closed in on one another, someone from the other group spoke.

"Where's my girl at?" they shouted out, with their faces still obscured by the darkness.

For a moment, all of us stayed perfectly quiet. As for myself, I couldn't tell if it was a diss or something else. Either way, I began to wonder how this was all going to end up. Then, suddenly, right out from beside me, Jane spoke up.

"Ted!" Jane screamed, suddenly dashing off to the crew in front of us.

She ran up and jumped up on one of them, hugging away, just like she had done earlier with me. After greeting each one of them, she then began talking away with them. As we were all now standing around, Ed, Mark, and I watched on, awkwardly, as Jane talked away with them, laughing on as they all too laughed away. As the moments rolled on, it was as if we had walked in on a family reunion of some family we never had once met. The three of us watched on as they all continued to laugh and joke around. Finally, after what seemed like a good five minutes, I looked over to Ed.

"What are you saying?" I asked, peering over at Jane and the others as they played on as if the three of us didn't exist.

"I think this is our cue to go," Ed said, looking over.

I nodded and then watched on for a few more seconds.

"Jane," I said, looking over as they all laughed and howled away. Despite my verbal shoulder tap, she just carried on, surely not even hearing me. Finally, after looking at both Ed and Mark, I tried again.

"Jane," I said again, despite the whole group of them carrying on. One of the crowd then perked up his head at me, clearly registering that I had called over. He then smirked and ducked his head back into the ensuing exchange. Seeing I was getting no help, I walked over to where Jane was.

"Jane," I said, waving my hand to get her attention.

"We're gonna go."

Jane turned her head.

"Oh, hey," she said, looking surprised as if she didn't even know who I was.

"Yeah," I continued.

"We're gonna leave," I said, looking at her.

"Say goodbye, Jane!" one of the guys from the crowd laughed out.

"Oh, okay," she said, quickly turning back to her group.

I stood there for a brief moment, then turned and walked over to Mark and Ed.

"Let's go," I said, not looking back.

The three of us walked along silently. The night streets were quiet, and all that could be heard was our footsteps on the road. The street lights shone down on us with their orange glow while our shadows changed directions with each streetlight that we passed. For a good ten minutes, not one of us said a word and just walked on. Then, finally, after some moments, Mark suddenly spoke.

"Hey," he began.

"Did you guys hear about that thing that's happening tonight?"

"Thing?" Ed replied.

"Yeah," Mark continued.

"The lunar eclipse."

"And it should be happening soon."

"Well, I dunno about you guys," Ed began.

"But I've felt eclipsed all day."

"Especially with those dudes who Jane ditched us for."

"I hope they get fuckin' eclipsed!"

"Hey, wait a minute," Mark cut in.

"I was thinking,"

"Aren't those dudes the ones who used to do break-ins?"

"You mean those guys that broke into the back of the Food City?" Ed replied, smirking.

"Yeah," Mark replied.

"Didn't they get caught because they trashed the place and ended up partying in it?"

"Oh fuck yeah!" Ed laughed.

"They fucked themselves because they just sat there and smashed all the shit,"

"What a bunch of douches," Mark replied, laughing away with Ed.

"Derek," Ed began, turning to me.

"Did you hear about that?"

"No," I replied.

"I didn't, but,"

"That's interesting,"

"What's interesting?" Ed asked, continuing to look at me. I paused for a moment as we continued to walk on in the quiet night. Then, after a few seconds, I replied.

"Oh," I began.

"I find it quite interesting."

"Interesting that they ruin things."

It took us only a handful of minutes before we arrived home. We then shook hands and parted ways for the night. Once I got in, I went down to do some rounds on the heavy bag. As I punched away, I thought all about the whole day. Finally, after hitting the bag with some good punches, I tired and decided to sit down. It was clear that my mind was too busy thinking about the whole day. But what I couldn't figure out was why it had such an impact on me. After all, it had just been another typical day, not unlike the rest. But for some reason, there was something about it all that didn't make sense. Or rather, maybe there was something that made sense about it, but it wasn't hitting me. Seeing this was the case, I decided to go outside for a walk.

As I walked along, I decided to go up to the top of a hill and find a suitable place to sit down. Once settled, I took a good look at the view before me. There, I looked on at all the usual buildings and landmarks off in the distance in the moonlight. In the daylight, they all had a familiar look to them, but now, in the moonlight, it looked like they belonged to another town altogether. As I sat looking on at the scene before me, I noticed that the light got dimmer. Looking up, I could only see a fraction of the moon, as now, the lunar eclipse was well underway.

Within seconds, I found myself sitting in almost complete darkness. And if things had looked different with just the moonlight, now, they looked very different, if they could be seen at all. The familiar buildings had once again taken on a different look than they had in the moonlight. Indeed, and most things were not even visible at all. I looked around for a bit, gazing at the scene before me, noting how the subtle moonlight had made such a difference. As I continued to look around, suddenly, up and out of nowhere, an intriguing line of thought hit me.

Like with the lunar eclipse, I, too, had been looking at the town using a dim kind of light. Thus, the dim light that I was using only revealed a part of what was really there. Only certain things were visible in this type of light. And after thinking more about it, there was a lot hidden from me with the light *I had been using* to view the town around me. I kept on thinking along these lines, all while sitting on top of the hill, in the darkness. And just as I thought on about it, it then hit me that this same idea also applied to the people I ran into that day.

The Dawn Of Enternity

Kuntala Bhattacharya

The Power of Solace preaches me
To conquer the vexation muddling me
The yearning for a selfless love
Perplexed to vanquish the disgrace.

Optimistic on the strengths of Almighty
Convinced on the potency and intensity
The mind anxiously desires a consolation
For a life uplifted into a world of elation.

Showers of thy blessings enraptures the soul
Enthralling the heart into a vivacious fold
Can I master my troubles and agonies?
Can I control my anguish and miseries?
A glimpse of positivity beckons me to its core
Dreams and aspirations gesture for luck galore

Towering through my sense of glory and happiness
Engulfing me within its lustrous manifolds.

The Dawn of "Eternity" arrives in splendor
A relief transforming oneself in ardor
Ushering in an era of limitless passions
Steering life into an aura of desires.

Dazzled by its royal grandeur
Gleaming within its illustrious wonder
My exuberant wishes magnify intensely
Longing for a world full of ecstasy.

Golden hues blush my inner self
Subtle charm captivates alluring oneself
Gesturing into an imperial ambiance
Enveloping a sphere of happiness and peace.

She Is A Poetry

Apoorva Batra

She is a poetry, a soulful poem.
A poem of light, yet covered with darkness.
A poem of mellifluous melody, yet trapped between deafs.
A poem of autumn, yet fallen for greys.

A poem of colours, but yet confused between shades.
A poem of nature, yet hiding from sunshine.
A poem of storm, yet searching a route to escape.

She is a poetry, poetry of love, but yet not fallen in love.
A poem of moon, but yet not shining.
A poem of night, yet to be filled with dreams.

She is a poetry of gold, yet to be infuse in fire.
She is a poem of mystery, yet to be solved.
A poem of mess, yet to be figured.
A poem of miracle, yet to be happen.
A poem of divinity, yet to be feel.

She is a poetry trapped in folded pages,
yet unsolved and unread mystery.

About the Authors

Vachaknavi Sarma aka Hiya is an automobile designer by profession. She belongs to the small town of Digboi, in the state of Assam in North-Eastern India. She presently lives in Washington DC, USA.

She writes poetry in her spare time. She has been writing for the past 8/9 years. Wild Imagination is her first publication. It is a collection of her very first poems. It is available worldwide on Amazon and various other websites.

She goes by the pen name of hiyasays

Find her on Instagram @*hiyaoxfordgirl*

James Kinsella is retired and lives in the USA. He worked as an IT Support Professional. Since his early school days, writing was always his love, so he decided to pursue this love when he retired. He enjoys writing and sharing his imagination with those who enjoy reading poetry and prose.

You could read his writings on Instagram

@jim.akinsel.1 or @jim.akinsella.1

Kuntala Bhattacharya, is an established IT consultant, writer, poet, and blogger.

Her articles, short stories, and poems have been published on many websites and have been appreciated by readers. Her books include *The Beautiful Lives, The Miraculous Discovery in the Woods, Treasures of Life* (published by Ukiyoto) and *Come and explore India with me* (published by Ukiyoto).

Born and brought up in West Bengal, she has always had a special fascination for literature. Her writing ventures in minimalistic form started from her college days. And then it continued to expand vividly, increasing her zeal to venture into the world of writers and poets.

Throughout her professional life, she has ventured into different places and interacted with people from different facets of life. Her innumerable experiences are reflected in her writings.

She likes using simple words for the benefit of readers of all generations. Her flow of words is smooth, often deliberating on the intrinsic aspects of the plot. She believes it is necessary to engage the readers at every moment in a story, without letting them have a feeling of boredom.

You can connect with her at :
1. *https://instagram.com/travelogue.of.kuntala* OR
2. *https://www.facebook.com/travelogueunlimited* OR
3. *https://www.instagram.com/big_book_barn/* OR
4. *Visit her website https://travelogueofkuntala.com*

Sanjana Chhatlani, is born & brought up in Mumbai & is a Finance Professional. She has Practiced & worked for last 15 years.

She has a flair for writing & has published her first fiction novel, a fun romcom by the name '**Twogether**' on kindle, the link to which is *https://www.amazon.com/dp/B08G86QCT2*.

She is also into writing Short stories & poems, both in English & Hindi.

She is learning Indian Classical music & has also composed Hindi songs & Bhajans. Her first, **Krishna – A Musical Odyssey,** a peppy fusion number is out on You-tube, Amazon Prime Music, Spotify, Apple music, etc. The you-tube link is:

https://youtu.be/VWVGTD_-tP8

She looks forward to recording more of her creations soon.

She is also an artist. Apart from graphite sketches, she also paints using different mediums like acrylics, water colours & inks.

She can be reached as under
www.instagram.com/saanchacreations
https://www.facebook.com/sanjanachhatlani
gmail : sanjana.chhatlani@gmail.com

Apoorva Batra (Cryptic Soul) is a Data Analyst by profession, Data Enthusist and likes to work and analyse data. She is MBA graduate and an Electronics enginneer she has just started her career as Data Analyst and working in an IT Company, she lives in a nuclear family alng with her mother, she is born in Ujjain and bought up in Indore, India.

She is a published poet, writer, painter, art and music lover. She likes to chant vedas and love reading books in several genre. She is writing from past 5 years with her pen name Cryptic Soul ,and got chance to publish her work in several books which are available on Amazon, she has also worked as Editor in an Indo - German poetry book which also is available on Amazon. She has also written technical articles for the technical blog. Ever since she has started writing , she has realised that along with this whole world, a parallel world resides within all of us , where we are the sun , the moon , and the solace we seek. She writes only to get peace. She is actively writing and posting content on her Instagram page known as '_Crypticsoul_'

She is a firm believer, she believes that life is a series of tiny miracles and we just need to notice them, we just need to enjoy the 'life' ride patiently. Everything that has happened , everything that is happening , and everything that is going to happen is destined , and we are walking towards tomorrow slowly, we humans are allowed to fall, allowed to make mistakes, but we must remember that we will rise and shine again like never before.

You can connect with her at -

1. *https://instagram.com/_crypticsoul_?utm_medium=copy_link*
2. *https://instagram.com/_apuurva_?utm_medium=copy_link*
3. *https://www.facebook.com/apurva.batra.94*

Pooja Natoo is a Literature Graduate. She is an avid reader and often loses herself in the musky scent of books. She loves old melodies alongwith a cup of chai.

She prefers poetry for all her expressions and is captivated by the glorious history of India, that is Bharat.

She has had her work featured in 3 anthologies and another one is going to be out soon.

She is compiling her first ever poetry collection- to stay connected and to interact, find her on Instagram: @love_and_solace

https://www.instagram.com/love_and_solace/

George Styles lives in Philadelphia, PA. He obtained his PhD in Biochemistry from the University of Ottawa in Ottawa, ON, Canada and is also the author of two books, "Chronic Calamity" and "Lost Without Mischief". He is currently working on his third book which is due out in Fall 2021.

Along with this, he has numerous hobbies including writing, song-writing, guitar and bass, martial arts, programming and coding, microcontrollers, reef aquariums, philosophy, and spends lots of time trying to decipher the universe and all its mysterious secrets.

Connect with George:

Twitter: *https://twitter.com/geostylegeo*

Instagram: *https://instagram.com/styles_george*

Facebook: *https://www.facebook.com/TheStylesG*

Blog: *https://geostylegeo.wixsite.com/thestylesg*

Elizabeth Anne Bryant is currently a social media manager in Northern Virginia.

She started writing poetry at the age of nine and loves imaging stories in her head.

She has a community on Instagram for writers and creatives on her page @lizthewritingwiz and is also an aspiring YouTuber on her new channel: Tutorial Queen.

She loves meeting new people and would love to hear from you on her Instagram or YouTube. She also wishes you a very wonderful day! Happy creating!

Dipannita Bhattacherya is a marketing professional and a freelance content writer and trainer. She takes immense pleasure in nurturing her hobbies so that her professional career doesn't make her a person concerned only with figures, data, statistics and profit and loss.

She is an ardent reader and traveller. She enjoys painting and writing short stories. She travels to a different world of colours and limitless imaginations through these activities. She enjoys expressing her emotions and thoughts through writing.

Her blogs have been published in some popular sites and writings have been published in some popular anthologies. She is inspired by the idea of 'art for art' and often paints or sketches based on a story, poem or song. That is what she has done for this book too.

She has had the opportunity to participate in art exhibitions held at renowned art galleries of Kolkata in India. She is also humbled by the opportunities to work for some of India's most eminent artists.

Check out her website https://www.monkatforty.com/

Connect with her at monkatforty@gmail.com

https://www.instagram.com/dipannitabhattacherya/

https://www.instagram.com/big_book_barn/

https://www.facebook.com/dipannita.bhattacherya

Soham Bhattacharya is a middle school student, passionate for drawing portraits, sketches, landscapes and traditional paintings.

His desire for art began since he was a toddler and continues to flourish more and more as he moves ahead in his life. He is the son of our author Kuntala Bhattacharya.

He supported our author Dipannita Bhattacherya in creating the artwork for the book "The Indigenous Compositions".

He can be reached at:

- *Creativityunlimited31@gmail.com* OR
- Youtube Channel – "My World of Art and Craft"

Johanny 'Joa' Ortega is proud immigrant who found a way to make space for herself through writing and recently podcasting. Raised in the Dominican Republic by her Abuela who inculcated in her a love of reading, Johanny grew up wanting to devour books and then write them. Eventually that love evolved into sharing knowledge with others through written and audio means.

You can find her plugged into her computer early in the mornings before the sun wakes up working on her debut, recording, editing or showing off her fur babies on IG & TikTok.

www.ingramcontent.com/pod-product-compliance
Lightning Source LLC
LaVergne TN
LVHW041220080526
838199LV00082B/1329